It Doesn't Have To Be Me

The stories in this collection were originally published in somewhat different form in the following: *Mother Jones, Powers of Desire, Confrontation, the minnesota review, Viva, Other Voices, Woman's World, The Cream City Review, Love Stories by New Women.*

Library of Congress Cataloging in Publication Data
It doesn't have to be me / by Carole Rosenthal
     p. cm.

ISBN 0-9654043-7-4 (paper)
     1. United States--Social life and customs--20th century--Fiction. 2. Women--United States--Fiction. I. Title.

PS3618.084 I85 20001
813'.6--dc21 2001016940

Manufactured in the United States of America

To Bob

It Doesn't Have To Be Me

BY CAROLE ROSENTHAL

H\s
HAMILTON STONE EDITIONS

CONTENTS

THE INDEPENDENT NOSE

It's taken all my life to come to grips with the fact that I'm a woman with a big nose. A long, sharp and slightly bent nose, bent at the crossroads as it were, forking to the right, indented, slightly scooped to the left. This comes from being broken by the outside flat of a hand belonging to a woman named Audrey who was in my Group Therapy, twisting her arms one night, uncoordinated in ancient anger towards her mother, who was no longer alive. Stuffed next to me on a nubby couch along a wall, Audrey squeezed shut her eyes and cried out, smashing me with a blind emotional backhand: "Take that, Mother! Take that!" An accident, fusing the narrow bone high, under the shallow of my left eye in one quick squeak and sliver of out-thrust bone. Almost immediately the nose and the valley of the eye went brackish, the color of algae.

"You broke my nose! You broke my nose!" I screamed, clapping my hands around it. I ran back and forth to the bathroom in the hall. I squinted in the mirror. Tears slid over my freckles. I whimpered, I cawed. "It hurts, it hurts."

Audrey pitched forward on the couch, a victim herself. She yelled, "I couldn't break your nose! I didn't. I'm not strong enough, I'm weak!"

The therapist's lip underslung, all wet and sparkly with excitement. He didn't believe in violence, but he liked the breakthrough way Audrey was standing up to me. "Mother transference," he said. "She needs her emotional space, too. Right?"

The next day, the nose that was mine seemed unrecognizably large, blooming unhealthily fat, swelling outward and upward, flourishing with color, bosky below the bridge, plugged up so that, below, nostrils pressed to their twin openings, sunken and concave. Ben, getting out of bed in the morning to see what was the matter at the mirror, looped a long supportive arm around my neck and told me not to worry, he didn't love me for my looks.

"What do you mean?"

He realized his mistake. "I think you're pretty anyway," he said, recovering.

Up the side steps to the hospital, through one door, loose and swinging, then another, he walked behind me, protective. Everyone in the emergency room stared at him: the nurse, the young doctors, the glossy receptionist who cocked her pixie head and asked me my insurance number, even the other patients, some of them doubled over and dripping blood. Beat her, he beat her, beat her, he beat her, they breathed. My nose was broken, glaring, splashy, but they were all looking at Ben. It hardly seemed fair.

"How did it happen?"

"An accident. Somebody was talking to me and gestured with their hand and hit me by accident," I told three people consecutively.

"Uh-huh, uh-huh." Raised eyebrows, raised pens. Flat eyes flick at Ben. He smiles. Oblivious.

"How did it happen?" Inside the intimate, beach blanket space of a curtained cubicle, the resident probes me firmly. None of your beeswax, Doctor. So what if I'm in therapy? You're probably fucked up, too. I go hot with explanation, shame and talky fear. If only I had a shorter nose, a Lady nose! I could roll back, search beneath those doctor eyes for lush fantasies, oh, lovely Lady, lovely, lovely Battered Lady. "X-rays?" he asks his friend, the other young doctor, across my nose.

They telepathize to one another with deep distaste. What a nose! A real schnoz, a peak of a beak! Smash couldn't help. Smash couldn't hurt.

Waiting for X-rays, Ben, who thinks of my face as friendly, my nose as an inseparable part of me, strokes my hand gently across his tall denim knee. I tell him I've decided to break Audrey's face, coming down her chimney at night and shattering her at the protruding point of her cheekbone, impossible to reconstruct without endless operations and plastic surgery. Audrey pinwheels with pain into the air of my mind, a dwindling sparkler on a Fourth of July night.

The cone of the big machine points. Fourteen X-rays come out, enough to give me leukemia or brain damage in some far away future, and the Doctor, as white and unforgiving as a porcelain autoclave sterilizer, tells me, "Nothing broken here. That nose is fine."

"But it's sitting smack under my eye!"

"I'm surprised you never noticed. It's obvious to me you have an off-center nose. It's been like that since you were a tiny child."

"It hurts, it hurts!"

"Pain is no indication." He snaps his finger against my see-through bone in shadowy black-and-white on the X-ray slab. "See, here's the calcification."

My mouth opens. My nose trumpets its rage.

Crazy lady. Ben pays the bill and takes me home, leaving with his shoulders high and wide, still respectable, unlike me.

In therapy where I'm trying to work through my anger at Audrey, the therapist flops forward on his elbows and looks sincerely into my eyes: "That nose was never straight to begin with. You have to learn to accept who you are."

"But my mother swears it was straight. She always told me I had a classical profile. Cleopatra, Nefertiti!" I weep.

"All mothers say that," he smiles comfortingly, enfolding his hands behind his neck, lowering his lids over tricks those mothers play. "Mothers!" he sighs. Oh, oh, what a job. . . .

By the end of the session I realize he's terrified I'm going to sue.

In the middle of our living room a life-sized drawing of me hangs over the sofa, me in my nightgown, bony legs askew, true to my rumpled and contradictory reality: a face divided by a Nose. Byzantine and ambiguous, one side friendly, the other slanty with suspicion. Who is looking, Friend or Foe? I look like my mother, and did even as a

child: Red Rover, Red Rover, let Kadey Come Over.
Then, nose-dive onto the cement between suddenly
unlinked arms, crash through the tricky opening to a
rough, sparkling, ultimate slab of sidewalk.   Black ants
walk by.   Little head, little thorax, little abdomen, little
wavy legs. Darkness and blood. I open my eyes. Look at
the walls, see all the pictures Ben has taken of Kadey? How
does she look?   Kadey smiling, Kadey sad, Kadey in con-
centration in close-up: see her nose? Well, what do you
think? Furrows of thought extend its length.

The stoplight at the Fifth Avenue corner near the New
School glows red.   I nudge Alexandra to a halt with my
shoulder. We're on our way home from statistics class.

"So they stick a thing like an ice-tea spoon up your nose,
holding you back, and re-position the shape.   It takes
maybe three visits.   I know because Dr. Raphael did it for
me when Alfie broke my nose."

"He broke your nose?"   I am incredulous, bowled over
to hear that her husband, the High Episcopal priest in a
collar, has clipped her precise upper-class nose.   Crossed
class lines.   Is no one safe?

"The British drink too much," she says, avoiding a taxi
that's inching up, sliding her eyes in peripheral judgment—
or am I the critical one now?   "Still, it's nobody's business
what we do in our home . . . ."

While I'm wadded up with cotton the plastic surgeon,
Dr. Raphael, smiles artistically, expensively, into my face.
His teeth gleam radiantly. His breath is warm and gentle.

"Would you like me to take off an inch or so while I'm at it? It could stand it, you know. Easy as pie in the hospital, as long as it's broken. Easily, yes, easily."

I rise as he advances, looking more and more like Audrey. "*My nose*, Doctor," I say with regal hauteur.

Whose voice is that?

My nose and I leave his office. We don't look back.

But at night I can't sleep because my nose is so big. I can barely breathe. It takes over my face, it almost suffocates in the pillows, it bumps into the walls. Ben says he can't even notice the difference. "You're so unvisual," I accuse. "So what?" he says: he loves me for myself. A wonderful trait. I know, I know. But who is myself anyway?

Each day as I age ever so slightly, my nose coarsens, hardening in its ways, longer and grosser, splotched with pores. Finally it develops allergies. Kleenex flowers litter our house. I take to bed, sighing under beautiful woodland sheets, leaves and flowers. The nose becomes fuller. I snuffle through it like a rooting beast, a curious boar, a frustrated ground critter searching out insects: I scoop with my sharp-axe, face down in the pillow, shoving my nose under rotting logs, into dark earth, unable to smell, poking what turns up. Curled slugs, discovered, re-shape themselves out of my path. The ground is moldy. The sheets need changing. But I can't tell the difference. My nose is no damned good, a prehensile relic. A shover and a blower. Frightening, naked, a fleshy jut.

Why do I have to accept it? Who says that I have to?

"I can't stand it, I can't stand it!" I sob one sleepless night, waking Ben, prodding him with its cartilage tip. "My nose is disgusting. Broken. Ugly. It doesn't even work."

"I don't think it is broken," he says sleepily, stretching out his hand from under the covers and patting me as if I'm a darling dog, an unruly high-strung pet who shares his bed. "That's not what the doctor said."

"It's like rubbery gristle," I moan. "All jaggy razor-blade bone."

"Go to sleep," he says, putting a pillow over his face.

I stick my head under the pillow next to his. "What's it good for?" I ask. He doesn't answer. His breath, moist and sweet like a summer lakeside, snores gently through his clear nose, rippling against me. But not pacifying.

I have a moment when I want to rush into the kitchen, pull open the door to the refrigerator, and stick my head into the freezer, lying with my cheek against the undefrosted ice until my nose freezes, goes numb, and then I snap most of it off. I'll heat the rest with an iron, or with my curling rod for my hair, re-molding it perky and sloping, still my nose after all, pressing it in and out and up—an impossibility. Finally I turn off the light. Feeling my alienation from it, I squeeze it between my thumb and forefinger.

A flash of insight: This nose is not Me.

This nose, sticking out so far into the world, so easily damaged, overly visible, so often broken and hurt, this nose has nothing to do with me. Stuck on my face, yes. Even heralding my presence, but that freak of fate doesn't make it mine. Or me responsible.

I wake Ben again, eager to tell him.

"What? Huh?" Then he agrees without opening his eyes. "Okay, it's not your nose," he says. "Too many things have happened to it, it's not your real nose, okay."

Sleepily, "Okay, okay." He thinks that by agreeing with me he'll make me happy. What an even-tempered man, but he isn't really helping. I can see there's a problem.

Now we've both disowned my nose. God, it's abandoned! Nobody loves it or claims it. How can it be answerable? My nose, uncared-for, can do whatever it wants.

"I want to go back to sleep," Ben whispers. He does. He rolls over on his stomach.

Like a primitive beast, my nose waits and waits. Until it's dark and quiet. Passing cars no longer flash their lights onto the ceiling. Then my nose attacks. Sheets bunch beneath Ben's wingbone when he arches. They drape over the ridges of his vertabrae, the smooth shallows of his flesh, all pink and ignorant like a baby. My hands clamp behind my back, my face swings down, almost drowning me in terror beneath the glutinous fibre of his muscles.

The nose stabs and stabs and stabs.

Poor despised, murderous nose. A victim of its past— hurt, angry, so brutalized and ignored, it turns on the only man who loves it, a senseless, random act of violence. The usual "underprivileged" story, a renegade nose in a society where a woman isn't even supposed to have a nose.

It subsides, twitching and tries to act anonymous, as if it belongs. I regard it almost with compassion. But not quite.

SHELLS

Dorrie got lost on her way home from having coffee with her friend Jennifer. Jennifer had just told her some shocking news.

"I know you suspected it anyway." She was having a love affair with Bryant, their mutual dentist. "I slept with him twice. It's so deep, the way we feel about each other. I broke it off because of Stan. Stan is furious at me. This affair is threatening to ruin my marriage. But being with Bryant has changed me. I can't let go."

"You told Stan?" Dorrie was shocked that at their age Jennifer regarded sleeping with a man as flirtatious as Bryant, who often flanked her with his thigh or brushed her breast by accident when she was reclining in the dental chair, as a serious affair.

"I had to, he could see I'd changed. That's what I need to talk to you about. Stan told me he talked to you when you called."

"But I called to talk to you and got Stan."

Or rather Stan got her, as so many other people did. Got her and told her things as if they thought she was wiser and more concerned with their well-being than she was—or at least than she wanted to be.

Dorrie, cautious, asked to hear more details before she gave Jennifer feedback on conducting her life. So what if Jennifer had a knack for getting into dumb situations? She realized now that Jennifer only wanted to meet her tonight after they finished teaching their painting classes to pick her brain about the weird phone conversation she'd had with Stan, a few hours earlier. Her friendship with Jennifer was at a tender intersection. After a casual five-year acquaintance, she had just crossed the threshold of her natural wariness to count Jennifer as a trustworthy friend. Beneath her open smiles and friendly appearance—all dyed reddish hair and many freckles—Dorrie imagined herself as a bit of a hermit crab, scuttling with stalk eyes and alert amusement through social situations, but holding her own secrets close, encased in a shell. She doubted that other people, particularly Jennifer, would be interested in her secrets. Her private life consisted of feelings and observations so hidden she sometimes felt like she was even keeping them secret from herself.

"What did Stan say about me?"

They were walking in the winter rain. Dorrie shrugged, reluctant to get in the middle of a fight between husband and wife. As usual, she wanted to hear Jennifer's story, but without seeming eager for it. The Soho streets were deserted. Jennifer's platform boots scuffed the sidewalk. She checked Dorrie's expression by angling sideways. Dorrie wiped cold drizzle off her glasses.

"If we're going to talk let's find a place to sit." She searched the side street for a coffee shop.

"Jennifer is very withholding," Stan had told her. Inappropriate, Dorrie thought, for someone she barely knew. All she had asked was a polite how are you, unleashing a torrent. "I guess you know we've been having problems." He didn't say what kind of problems but he was fishing to find out if Jennifer had already confided in her; if so, how much she knew. "We've been thinking of bagging it . . . ." His tone annoyed her. *Poor me, I'm being cool*—a monotone. "Our marriage, I mean."

Dorrie was silent. She pictured somebody stuffing Stan and Jennifer into a poacher's bag, rushing through woods.

"Withholding?" she sucked in breath. Exciting information but dangerous territory. Squalling partners re-united. Whatever you said could be turned against you. Her own husband would never talk about her to anybody behind her back. Matthew didn't even talk to her anymore. He just came home from work, pulled on denim cutoffs, and read the design journals. Wherever she was sitting, she could count on him to settle himself somewhere else, across the room. So in spite of herself, she felt a tug of pity for Stan. "Jennifer is always generous to me as a friend."

"As a friend, yes. I'd love to have her as a friend. But as a wife, no. If a man is with a woman he's looking for something in himself, but Jennifer isn't fulfilling that role. And she doesn't bring in any money either. It would help if she'd get a better job . . . ."

A disturbing call. Too convoluted, some kind of psychobabble. Dorrie knew he and Jennifer were in couples therapy together. She'd only met Stan twice, but the few times she'd seen him perform in clubs she admired his music.

"Isn't Jennifer at home?"

"No, she's out. She's always out to me lately. Even when she's home I can't get through."

Stan played alto sax and clarinet and innovated global boogie on found instruments like strands of seashells, and coffee pots, and ploughshares from his uncle's farm. He was an intense red-faced burly man Dorrie found hard to talk to. He didn't listen, he only riffed. If she and Jennifer hadn't been getting chummier in the last six months, maybe she would have hung up right away. For the sake of her friendship she was putting her friendship in jeopardy. Did that make sense?

"But I do know a good place for sitting around here," Jennifer said to Dorrie. "A coffee place near—where are we? On Broadway and Bleecker? It's called . . . wait, wait . . . . I'll think of it!" She spun around excitedly, like a kid. Her silvery rain-cape flared. Her voice was high and slender. So was Jennifer. She'd smoked a joint in the studio bathroom on their way out. She didn't act like a married woman of forty. Nobody did these days. Jennifer still pictured herself as a bad girl, the risk-taker in whimsical rhinestones and vintage hats, the girl she used to be, but wasn't now. Her shadow shimmered in a puddle under a street-light.

Dorrie watched her own shadow, next to it, squashed into a puffy nylon rain-shell, edging sideways. She looked like a crab, all right; next to Jennifer, she looked skinny-legged and squat.

"There it is! The *Résumé Cafe*," cried Jennifer.

They crossed the street. The cafe was pink, warmly lit. A waitress showed them to a tiny table wedged between four young men in dress shirts and ties playing bridge with jackets slung over their chairs, and a group of slouching arty types in silks who didn't seem to be speaking to each other.

"I'm embarrassed, I don't know where to start," Jennifer said. Like a kid, she started to cry.

The bridge players were drinking lattes; at the other table they glanced away.

"It's hard to talk when we're so hemmed in." Dorrie turned to look behind her, protective. Maybe somebody was paying a check? She didn't want eavesdroppers on Jennifer's confessions.

Dorrie spotted an empty corner booth and suddenly remembered that during the first years of her marriage she'd been to this cafe, and sat in that very booth. Back when she and Matthew used to go places to be alone together, the two of them making running commentaries about everybody and everyplace—as if the rest of world were a movie being put on for their benefit. The good old days. The good old narcissistic days, Matthew always called them disdainfully when she mentioned them now.

"Let's move," Dorrie said, carrying her place setting and glass of water back to the booth.

Jennifer followed, brandishing her cutlery in the air like a sword. The waitress swabbed down the table with fast sullen jerks. She was irritated by the switch.

The cafe, Dorrie vaguely recalled, had had a different name back then.

Jennifer plunked forward on her elbows. Her face, round-eyed and classically oval, turned hideously long and beseeching as a question burst out.

"What do you do when you're not sexually compatible with someone you live with? Stan and I have been married for seven, almost eight years, and I know you and Matthew have been together even longer than that. How do you make it work?"

"Matthew and I are compatible," Dorrie said quickly. She always froze on the subject of her own sex life. The fragility of intimacy. It needed protection. Besides, nothing quirky—not that she was telling a lie.

She could tell that Jennifer was trying to hide her disappointment. Clearly she'd hoped to find Dorrie in the same pickle. A twist of guilt told Dorrie she owed Jennifer some dirty tidbit now.

"I know you're happy. That's why I wanted to talk to you. I want to talk to you *because*," Jennifer stressed the word, eyes at half-mast, "you're in a happy relationship, and *because*," she raced past her embarrassment, "you know Bryant and so you can understand at least that part of my problem. Remember, you said he was a wonderful dentist. You recommended him to me, in fact." She peeked out slyly under long blonde bangs. "And I know you said that you were charmed by him too."

"He is charming," Dorrie said, firmly. Abruptly she remembered what the cafe had been called. Something hip back then. *The Naked i.*

What charmed Dorrie most about Bryant was not his jokey manner or long-lashed eyes, nor even his dimples or athletic grace. All of these were characteristics which Dorrie recognized as conventionally charming but they vaguely alarmed her, like static-filled air. Rather, Dorrie was charmed by Bryant's egotism and scattershot chatter. Dorrie enjoyed his brooding, which was more revealing than he knew. Perhaps because he'd projected some kinship onto her sympathetic passivity over the years ("Open, please . . . Wider, please . . . Thank you . . ."), Bryant had taken to sharing his career doubts with her, strange musings.

"The angst of dentistry! It's a terrible profession. Do you know that dentists have the highest rate of suicide of any profession except psychiatry?"

"Why i*sh zh*at?" Bryant hooked a de-salivating device over her lower teeth, wadding her molars with cotton. He stepped back to admire his handiwork.

"Because dentists cause people pain. Everybody hates us. It takes a toll."

But everybody probably didn't keep up their end of the gape-mouthed dialogue like Dorrie did after she noticed how much Bryant craved instant appreciation and sympathetic responses. It excited her to keep him talking, examining him in close-up, just as he was examining her.

"Bu*h sh*o do doctor*sh*," she tried to smile.

"Totally different. Doctors have glamour. People think of dentists as frustrated sadists and control freaks who've found a socially acceptable outlet for their anal aggressions. Nobody takes a dentist seriously. It's all dentists talk about when we get together at parties. How we're the butt of bad jokes. Imagine what it must be like at a proctologist's convention."

"Ouch!" She couldn't help squirming.

"Did I hurt you?" He looked annoyed. "Your teeth are shifting from age. Mouths change."

She focused on a Daumier print of a grotesquely grinning dentist applying a pliers to a cringing patient. The pain intensified. He poked as if her teeth were shifting, behaving shiftily right now under his dental tools. She switched to a narrow view of the East River out the window, gray and serene.

His voice was taking on a gruff edge, confidential, too personal despite his flirtations, for such a noncommittal room.

"Take me, for instance. Most dentists don't start out to be dentists . . . . Wider, please . . . ."

She looked up his nostrils, clipped nose hairs her immediate view. She suddenly imagined putting together a small grid-like series of quivering nostril paintings based on Bryant. They would hang next to her recent hermit crab canvases. His nostrils would flare pink and vein-y, pressing foggily against the glass. Her latest idea was for paintings that all caught parts of people, frozen, defenseless, off-guard.

Then Bryant told her again how he'd gone into dentistry as a safe profession his parents would support when he was in college and the woman who would become his first wife got pregnant. "I used to want to be a writer, or an intellectual. But the mind is over-rated," he said, winking, pressing close. She minced him mentally, and envisioned her paintings. Question-mark shaped ears, a smirk, albumininous eyes.

Shadows flickered on the pink walls of the cafe and Dorrie felt her breath rise and snag as, without warning, Jennifer began describing the sexual byplay of her two nights with Bryant.

Jennifer said, "He stuck a flashlight up my vagina and handed me a mirror. It was incredible. Don't tell a soul."

Dorrie pictured Bryant commanding Jennifer to open her thighs (" . . . Wider, please . . ."). That made her blush.

"It's too warm in here, Dorrie. Maybe we should tell the management to turn the heat down. You're breaking out in blotches." Jennifer swung around, signalling for the waitress.

"Probably early hot flashes," Dorrie joked.

"But you see my problem? It's like what you said about Matthew the other day, that you're growing faster than he is."

Immediately, Dorrie was sorry she'd said it. No waitress materialized.

"At least Matthew gives you room," Jennifer said. "I
mean, Stan is always pushing himself on me with his needs.
It's such a cliché. After so many years, Stan and I are more
like friends. Now he wants to become friends with Bryant
so he can understand why I'm involved with him."

Dorrie tucked her legs under the booth. She felt safe in
the booth. It shamed her to remember how she'd been flattered and a little bit frightened by her enforced intimacy
with Bryant. She remembered visualizing the inside of her
mouth from his point of view—slimy ripe cavern of pleasure, sex and food, aggression and pain.

"That's a bad idea."

"I know. Bryant thinks we ought to cool things down,
for my sake. He's taking the blame because my marriage
went rocky. I'm not so sure. Most marriages have some
rocks in them, don't they?"

Dorrie said nothing. She imagined Matthew in bed by
this hour, checking the clock. Waiting for her? Fat chance.
When he finally visited her studio last week after one of his
big client preparations, Dorrie was eager to show him the
hermit crab series, explaining in what she soon saw was too
much detail how hermit crabs, with age, grew too bulky for
their acquired shells and literally suffocated if the shells
weren't cast off—yet without shells their soft bodies were
completely exposed.

"Catch 22, it isn't safe either way, so they only leave if
they're suffocating or in order to mate. Sort of like long-term
relationships," Dorrie had joked, trying to hold Matthew's
flagging interest by lobbing him an opportunity for easy irony
at her expense. But he was already turning away.

She pictured him now reading in bed, wrapped in a blanket, Navajo-style, his oversized bluff of a forehead, his
thick sandy eyebrows and bushy moustache. They had met

twenty years ago as art students. But Matthew molted
from being a fine artist into an advertising design director
for a national magazine. She hadn't told him she was going
out with Jennifer tonight.

She shot Jennifer an encouraging smile.

Jennifer said, "See, if I separate from Stan it will be like
starting all over again. Maybe that's a good thing."

"Are things bad enough with Stan that you're actually
thinking about it? Do you think Bryant actually wants you
to break up your marriage?"

She was resentful of Jennifer's intensity; she knew other
women Bryant had slept with. Little bubbles of annoyance
boiled upwards in her mind. She didn't want to come right
out and tell Jennifer this starcrossed relationship with
Bryant was all her fantasy. Listen, she told herself, most
reality is fantasy. It was the promise of the fantasy she was
envious of. Ever since Matthew realized that he was never
going to be the famous artist he once dreamed himself to
be, the next Matisse, the next Franz Kline, not even the
next Julian Schnabel of his generation—an artist he had
contempt for, but whose wealth and high recognition fac-
tor he secretly envied—he had retreated from Dorrie's, and
everyone else's, aggressive ambitions for him, and eventu-
ally—although she couldn't pinpoint when—from himself.

"Maybe Bryant doesn't want the responsibility of a relationship," Dorrie snapped.

Jennifer recoiled as if Dorrie was pinching her.

Instantly, Dorrie felt bad. Jennifer's situation was serious
in spite of being ridiculous.

"It's true, he has a lot of responsibilities," she said, deliberately vague—pretending to misunderstand.

Dorrie felt as if her skin was too tight.

"You should see how red your face is turning," Jennifer said, squinting dreamily, as if thrilled by her own powers of perception. "Don't you hate the way skin changes at our age? My own skin is so sensitive too."

"*Excuse me, ladies—*"

A young waiter in clunky hipster glasses suddenly swooped his delicate face in between them. He was cute. Smiling, shiny, unlike their own scowling waitress. He wore a tiny earring that looked like a fishing lure, and displayed a carefully tended three-day stubble.

Dorrie scooted sideways.

"Did you lose these?"

He dangled Dorrie's big purse and a pair of earmuffs in front of their eyes.

"My purse! Did you just find it?"

"Oh, god, we left all our things at the last table when we moved."

The cute waiter laughed, delighted.

"We're so dumb," said Jennifer, snatching at the earmuffs. "These belong to me."

Dorrie felt fluttery. The waiter was leaning towards her, close to her face. The air was roiling. "How did you know this purse was mine?" She wondered why their waitress hadn't found it.

"By going through your wallet, trying to find a phone number. I found the video club card with your husband's name on it and I looked him up. I would have recognized you from your driver's license if you hadn't changed your hair color."

"You called my husband?" Dorrie was startled, then excited by the intrusion. She felt light-headed at the image of a stranger curiously slipping his fingers through her credit cards, appointment slips, paint receipts and birth control pills. "Oh, thank you. Thank you so much."

She breathed into his face. He breathed back, and she got scared.

"But I'm worried that my husband will worry since you called him. I'd like to tell him you found me. Do you have a phone?"

"You don't have one with you? There's a public phone across the street."

She felt ashamed that there was no one for her to be urgently available to, and that she didn't carry her own mobile phone.

"Matthew's got the flu bug or something," she said to Jennifer, pointedly turning her back on the waiter. There was a phone on the cashier's desk in the front of the restaurant, and she took the cute waiter's response as rebuff. "I don't want Matthew to bundle up and run down here to retrieve my purse for me."

"That's what I mean," Jennifer sighed. "You have such a caring relationship with Matthew. It's what I'm missing most with Stan."

In front of an old tenement building, alone, Dorrie huddled under the kiosk.

It was wet on the street, coming down cold. The first call reached a wrong number. She dialed again.

"Matt?"

Matthew was asleep already, just as she'd thought. He often fell asleep in bed, still sitting up. Beside him would be a half-filled snifter of brandy, miraculously unspilled. The snifter of brandy was his ritual equivalent of a child's cup of steamy cocoa before bedtime, his comfort cue before letting go. He sounded distant, gurgly on his end of the phone, like someone inhabiting another element without any memory of this one, sunken into himself and far away.

"I called the studio to let them know where your purse was, in case you went back," he said.

"It's funny the waiter called you though, isn't it?"

"Funny? How come?" His voice was blank.

"Because these days it seems like I'm always losing things." Her voice slipped out small, almost seductive, like something that could fall between cracks. She wanted a moment of intimacy with him, and thought maybe by making fun of herself she might establish it. He'd teased her that morning about misplacing the Visa bills. She remembered when she wouldn't have had to explain her sense of humor. Back then he and Dorrie thought everything everybody else did was funny—or at least worth commenting on.

"Matthew, let's do something spur-of-the-moment together. Meet me on the corner of Broadway and Bleecker? That's the *Résumé Cafe*. It's a little place where we used to go. It'll be fun to do something new and spontaneous, like we used to."

"Something old then, you mean. Going backwards. I'm not dropping into a place that invites credentials. Have you seen the weather? You're out of your mind if you think I'm going out on a night like this. I have a big meeting—"

"Matthew, please. I'm standing outside in the weather right now. Please don't say no to me."

Back in the old days, she used to marvel at every little detail about Matthew, the deepset eyes, his strangely ridged fingernails, his carefully composed emergency crisis kit that he kept in each of the bathrooms, and at their lives together.

"Anyway, I just called you because I didn't want you to worry about me."

"Why should I worry about you when you can take care of yourself?"

She hung up the phone and a sensation she couldn't quite identify swelled up in her so fast that she felt unwieldy, too big for her skin which felt foreign, a carapace, and she thought she heard a crack. She exerted a fierce effort to hold herself down, down, down. Who was that loving husband about whom she earlier pretended to be so silently boastful, so misleadingly smug? She blinked at something tiny and naked crawling away from the phone down the wet sidewalk.

When she returned to the hot cafe and Jennifer's urgency, Dorrie announced Matthew's flu bug was getting the better of him, and that she had to go.

Dorrie left a big tip and she and Jennifer split the bill.

Jennifer seemed to be afloat in the air. "It's so beautiful out. Look, can you see all the rainbow halos from the moisture under the street lamps? This was a good conversation for me, it helped."

They flagged a cab. It splashed Dorrie when it came to a stop. She decided to walk home anyway since she and Jennifer were traveling in opposite directions. The sleet blew into her face. Strange, the slicing moisture felt good. She took off her blurring glasses. Now she could barely see. What would she say to Stan the next time she called Jennifer if he picked up the phone? Crazy to worry about it, but she didn't want to get caught in the middle. Stan could distort her noncommittal responses, interpret them for or against.

A glum disappointment clung, despite the wind. But she wasn't disappointed in Bryant. She laughed out loud, open-mouthed, at the fact that he, a good dentist all right with a soupçon of charm but a bit of a fool, was the only person tonight who hadn't let her down. The wind blew against her teeth. She pictured Bryant in the room in which their narrow controlled relationship took place. She couldn't picture him outside it, she realized, not even with Jennifer.

She chose a new route home, a route down side streets, dark brick-canyoned ones where she passed an obsolete-looking diner and a rug warehouse with a gleaming show-case that she'd never seen before. Then she saw strangers laughing, slinging their arms around each other, clumping out of a movie complex. Where was she now? Everything looked odd and looming without her glasses. But being lost didn't feel unnatural or scary, or like she was in the wrong place. For all she knew, the way life changed anyway without warning despite her best efforts—skin, teeth, marriage, friends—this place she didn't recognize might be her home now even though she couldn't read the street signs.

SWEEPING THE FUTURE CLEAN

The back room was full of clothes, jam-packed into closets and chests, and dust. Too many clothes, too many sizes, from 7 to 11. Nina's past and future expectations, in styles long and short. A raucous display, a cacophony of colors and costumes and possibilities. She hated to give up the possibilities, despite her new husband's urging, even though she wanted to please him.

She said, appealing, "You never know what a person might want or need. Styles come back. They do, you know."

"Yeah, every twenty years," he said, grinning, leaning into the door frame, tall and unimpressed, a good-looking dark haired man who liked fresh starts. "Maybe once in a generation."

She stalled for time with a question. "Is a generation really that long?"

"Come on, Nina. Breaking old habits would be good for both of us. What do you have to hang on to everything for? Let's take a practical step here. How about if we throw only things you haven't used in a year into the garbage, all right?"

"Into the garbage? Oh, hey! Wait a minute! Wait, wait. . . ."

But his arm had already stretched out towards the sliding closet and she had to grab it down by the fingers.

She couldn't know the future, so how could he? What if a thing they discarded together turned out to be just the thing she ought to keep?

Old habits. Family memories. The question was should she change for him or should she not?

"Will it last?" her mother had asked her six weeks ago, long-distance, when she found out that this would be Dennis's fourth marriage, habitually worrying about Nina's actions because Nina was the baby of the family, even though Nina too had been married more than once.

"What a question," Nina laughed, coiling black telephone wire around her thumb. "Dennis and I certainly need to have trust and faith in each other that it will."

After the no-frills wedding, driving out of the city overnight to visit her parents—an old-fashioned suburb in Vermont, wide streets overhung with maple trees, big houses straight-laced with fences, a yard busy with a barking dog—Nina hugged her new husband's arm, happy that her past and future would finally meet.

Her mother, still beautiful for her age, white curls floating on top of brown curls, was nervous at meeting the new husband, who reached out formally in greeting and shook her hand. She rushed around the living room plumping pillows behind their backs, balancing coffee cups, and weaving in and out of columns of cardboard boxes that formed labyrinthine paths, boxes that have always been there, Nina explained later, only not so many.

"Are you planning to move somewhere?" Dennis had asked her father.

"No, why, no," her father had said, surprised. Her parents were savers. She had forgotten to mention this to Dennis.

Downstairs the cardboard boxes lined the walls, obscuring family portraits. Upstairs, the boxes neatly labeled— Garden Club projects, School Reports, Birthdays, juicers and Cuisinarts and gadgets bought in duplicate in case of weddings—had taken over since the last children moved away. They remolded space, creating trails that narrowed, that diminished height and thickened unexpectedly, clogging and hardening the house. There was furniture too, tables resting on top of other tables, bentwood legs overlapping wicker stubs, chairs cradling other smaller chairs. They bricked and bric-a-bracked the room solid until . . . Surprise! "What?" . . . Some rooms are no rooms at all!

"Do you think there's any room for us to sleep?" her new husband had asked over dinner, an excessive disarray of food.

"Don't be silly!" she calmed.

But the bedroom her parents offered was mercifully free of boxes. And the bed was very aristocratic, a Princess-and-the-Pea-type bed, Nina thought, although a little high and close to the ceiling, three mattresses resting on top of a box spring. ("We just cleaned out the twins' room for storage. You can't throw perfectly good Posturepedics away!")

"But I can't sleep up there with that thing on the bed," Dennis said while he was undressing, hanging up his shirt. He pointed to a tall wooden frame, an antique map of the world with rusty waterstains, standing upright on the bed, resting against the wall.

"We'll pull the bed out and slide it to the floor," Nina suggested.

But the frame slipped from her hand and fell into the dark crevice. Not just a crash. A long, tinkling crunch.

"What's that?"

Nina knelt. Dennis's family was never poor, never hoarded against disaster, he didn't understand. She poked her head under the ruffled bedskirt. Gleaming like cracked eggshells, in thin curves, were lightbulbs, and long neon ribbons in and out of paper wrappers.

Dennis's mouth dropped. "They don't waste a space!"

The next morning, while toast was stacked on the kitchen table and her parents still slept upstairs, Dennis flipped up the butter bin, and said, "Look here!"

She squinted at five, six, no, *seven*, ends of butter saved next to a fresh stick.

"For cake pans, naturally," she said to him, defensive. "Look, my parents love each other. This is a happy home."

Dennis shook his head. Two different worlds. Strain forced him to revert to familiar New York vernacular.

"*Shmateh* butter," he cried. "Even in the refrigerator, leftover junk, junk, junk . . . ."

"Why does it have to be such a big deal?" Dennis said, shrugging, holding up the plastic trash bags, but still leaning against the door. "Why can't we just go through the closets and the shelves together and throw out everything you don't use anymore?"

Nina looked skeptical. Still. Watching as he stood, thin and elegant in the lamplight with the shiny empty trash bags draped over his angled arm like a couturier or a decorator. No, like a mannikin, someone's fantasy, an idealized fill-in-the blank Rorschach test man, so straight-jawed, so poised.

"All right?"

But he was eager to spring into action. Finally she relented, thrilled that he was willing to help her, frightened and excited by the thought of his stripping that cluttered room bare, by the thought that between the two of them, perhaps, in that extra room she'd been using to stash her history, they could make a fresh start, a place that could mean anything, a precise white-on-white room, dusty only with silver shadows, no piles, no heaps. A room so clear and sparkling that it had see-through bookshelves, glass tables, lucite chairs, a Cinderella's slipper-type room that would both reveal and transform her.

"I love you," she said.

"I love you, too."

She nodded. She trusted him.

He smiled. "Okay?" In fact, once he received her word, he whirred into action like a cleaning machine, a magic suction, a householder's dream, pulling her clothes out of the closet as if by will—all sizes, all colors. Purple and pink and rust and green, dispersing them into a rising pyramid on the floor. Fast hands, fast feet, fast eyes. Faster than she was, too fast for her to bear.

"Wait! Wait—"

Out of the drawers, off the shelves, out of the crannies, unzipping wardrobe bags, under cracks. Clothes! Books! Papers! He points. Scat! Scat!

"*Wait! Wait!*"

She spotted a striped knit that almost fit her, just five pounds more, no, well, maybe ten. But she loved that outfit. *Wait!* A turquoise blue silk, bias-cut. "*I bought that for*

*Julie's last wedding. Stop! I was the matron of honor, don't
you care?"* She fell on top of it. Then a khaki raincoat,
three sweaters, a sequined shawl.

Wait! That jacket is half of a suit. Wait, wait . . . .

Graduate school biology notes ("You've changed careers,
you're never going to use them again . . . ." , anti-nuclear
power buttons ("That plant is already closed!"). She was
on her hands and knees on the floor trying to recover the
promises of the past, who she was, who she could have
been. Snatching them back, refusing to give them up.
Faster and faster, all fingers and teeth and claws. A box of
travel mementoes, old beads, two books . . . .

But he was faster than she was. Spinning efficiently, back
and forth, and all around. She couldn't keep up, though
she was sweating now, draped in the costumes she was rescuing, layers on heavy layers, bobbing up and down like a
kid at Halloween. She ducked. She sputtered. *This is
mine, and so is that.* But there went Dennis with the first
trash bag, twisting the tie, skinning her of possessions, taking away her just-in-case, winking, and patting her on the
head. Out the door, down the steps, and clicking his heels
down the marble hall.

Then he was back again, smiling and unencumbered.
Whew! She couldn't even see what he was taking—

"Wait, Honey! Please, wait . . . ."

But he didn't wait, he just strolled into the closet, filling
another dark bag, packing another load downstairs, helpful
but firm.

"Good God! Where did you get all these clothes? How
did you have so many to begin with? You always seem to
wear just the same few things."

Her feelings were hurt. He was panting.

Afterwards, he draped his arm around her, smoothing dust swivels from her skin, leading her into the bathroom and lathering her white with his hands. Remolding. Then he took her by the wrist and drew her into their bedroom, telling her she looked lovely to him and so fresh. "This is for us."

"I adore you," Nina smiles happily.

"And don't you feel better with all this space around you now?"

The next morning, she was standing in the center of the suddenly large and extra room, empty and rejected-looking with its drawers and closets hanging open, when her old boyfriend Raymond, a film-maker, called her on the telephone.

"Go to the side of your living room and look out your window," Raymond said. "Man, talk about cultural divisions, this is an instant study in cultural anthropology for *Natural History* magazine, I only wish I had my video camera out of hock. Unbelievable, it's unbelievable, I see it as a PBS special, maybe with lots of quick-cuts, the theme of recycling, the relationship between roles, social status and ecology, right? Go on, I'll hold on, go see what I mean!"

Nina laid the phone down on the kitchen counter and went into the living room, leaning on the window ledge and looking down beneath the apartment, beneath the stripped winter branches of the trees. She saw a carnival of colors criss-crossing the cement. Her throwaways, pulled from the unlocked cul-de-sac at the building's side. Four figures were battling over them. A tall rawboned women with tufty gray hair who stacked and racketed her clothes into a wire shopping cart—a homeless woman who lived in neighborhood doorways and filled vestibules with yeasty fumes—two down-at-heels men who were vendors regularly narrowing the sidewalks of her street by creating late-night flea markets, and a slo-mo junky. The junky squeezed between them rattling his discovery, a bottle of unused pills, plucked out of one of Nina's pockets.

"It certainly is unbelievable," Nina agreed when she came back on the telephone. Yet unbelievable wasn't exactly the word she felt. Confusing. Unsettling. Creepy. "But how did you know that those things were mine?"

Raymond laughed, a series of derisive hiccups. "I met Dennis on the street last night when he was carrying out the bags. Besides, Pal O' My Heart, we lived together for a long time. Don't you think I know you?"

Later Nina forced herself to go in and take measurements off one wall of the extra room. An extra room seemed like a piggy privilege suddenly. Every once in a while she glanced out of her living room window. More people came to pick over her things. Art types, scavengers for resale, vintage mavens, hard-core punks. She watched as they examined for rips, for style, one or two of them holding clothes up against their bodies, checking for fit or swatches—then stuffing their take into bags, like poachers. But as the day darkened, more and more of her clothes were left behind. The colors and shapes seemed less gala now, more bedraggled. *This one?* NO! *That one?* NO, NO! These costumes had a discarded life of their own. Finally she went downstairs and folded what was left and trampled into the plastic coverings. But someone must have come after her and emptied the bag again. When it snowed that night, she imagined high drifts of cold white nestled on top of the limp unprotected cloth. Yet by morning, all had been stripped away.

Nina was coming out of the supermarket, planning a splurge of dinner menu in her head because she'd come upon an exceptionally good rack of lamb on sale, when she ran into somebody so familiar that she immediately broke into a wide smile of recognition. The welcoming exuberance was already out of her mouth and she had already jogged her grocery bag onto her hip, extending her hand, before she realized that she was grasping the shabby arm of the tall, rawboned shopping-cart lady—who looked so warm and familiar because her entire tufty head was encased right down to the bristles in Nina's favorite feather and hand-crocheted hat. The red wide-brimmed hat. The very hat whose pattern she had designed as one of her more inspired Christmas creations last year, when even Dennis insisted, "It's quirky, but it's got a lot of personality. It's you." Only now its dashing embroidered back and featherwork was worn forward and its soft brim was rolled behind.

"What do you want?" the shopping cart lady asked loudly. She seemed to think that Nina was threatening her.

Nina backed up to apologize, to explain. "It's the hat, my hat. You see, I made it myself."

"You fuckface, you fagbag! No, not yours! It's my hat. No, it's mine." The shopping-cart lady flung her hand out fast, as if striking for a principle, but her fist landed on top of her own head where she clamped the red hat tight. She angled her body fiercely towards Nina.

Nina leaped sideways to avoid her, frightened. The wire cart filled with clothes was standing directly behind Nina.

Her hip bumped the cart hard and she lost her balance. She fell, and the groceries toppled out of the bag and splayed around her in the snow, where they rocked crazily and made zigzag tracks. The shopping-cart lady ran behind her and raced the wobbling cart to safety down the street.

A man stopped. A neighbor. A Salvadoran restaurant worker INS had come searching for last month. He reached for an elbow and helped Nina up. She brushed herself off, shaken, and embarrassed. She started walking home. But at the stoplight she turned and came back to collect her groceries from the street. Then she took a cab to the apartment and climbed in bed.

That night, when Dennis came home, she kept watching him while he was eating dinner, the quick gleaming movement of his knife and fork, the neat way he picked apart his food, discarding the fat and the bones. He wouldn't have thrown her red hat away on purpose, he admired it, he'd told her it was a work of art. It must have been tucked into the folds of her old khaki coat, or maybe caught up in the haste. But it made her queasy anyway. Uneasy, uncertain of him. When they finally went to sleep, she had a dream about her parents: they crouched on the green summer lawn next to the lilac bush in front of the house, crowded out by the bounty of boxes and furniture and possibilities they had saved. She woke early and tried to re-structure the dream, to dream it again to make events come out this time with a happy ending.

Dennis rolled over sleepily and reached out for her with his warm hand.

"I love you, Honey," she said into the side of his neck.

"I love you, too."

"I'm glad I threw things away finally, I don't have to hold on to everything just in case, for the future." After all, even in her dream at least her parents still had each other, she thought guiltily—though it seemed rotten that some people and not others always had the opportunity to pick and choose.

"You can't hang on to everything, Nina. Times change. Evolution. Progress. It's unrealistic to think that you can."

Evolution? She thought about the world outside her window.

Her heart paled, tightened. "Times do change, you're right. But what if something happens? What if one of us needs more than the other can give, or makes a mistake?"

"Good grief, we've been married for less than six months and you're starting that already. Why do you always have to look at the unpleasant side of everything?"

He sounded impatient. The alarm rang.

"Don't be ornery. I really am glad that you made me get rid of things I don't need," her voice said. "It's disgusting to hold on to everything." She hadn't told him yet about the hat. "I am glad about that, I really am."

But despite what she was saying, when he tried to roll over to push in the alarm-clock buzzer, it startled her to notice her fingernails digging into his arm. And looking down at the way she was twisting his skin, actually crumpling it, she saw that he was shocked too. Suddenly she felt crowded. Still, she was hanging on.

THE RED PLASTIC GUN

I turn off the television and sit, watching the luminous spot in the center of the set grow smaller. Then, still holding a can of Diet Pepsi, I lean over, pressing my nose to the window screen, and watch the shadowed people of the city walk through the gray and hazy summer streets. The heavy air flickers. A thin rain is falling through it. I blink, and behind my darkened lids test patterns jump.

Poor reception. Getting static.

My husband buzzes his shaver in the bathroom. I'm getting impatient. "Hurry, Michael," I yell. "It's beginning to rain!" We're taking a walk this afternoon because our air conditioner is on the blink and our apartment is particularly oppressive.

"Ready?" Michael calls, coming into the living room with a blue towel tossed across his shoulder.

"Ready," I reply.

He grabs a shirt hanging on the knob of the door and I grab my pocketbook, and we both say goodbye to the cat. Then we start down the damp, echoing (but very clean) marble steps and go out into the street.

New York streets smell in summer. Odors packing together like foam rubber, stuffing up the front of your nose and expanding. Both Michael and I are breathing through our mouths.

First we hold hands for about a block, but soon that feels clammy; we're sticking to each other. Then we drop our arms to our sides where they barely move at all, as if encased and protected from their own thrust by the padding of the heavy air.

"Michael," I call to him, "let's begin to play." He can hardly hear me, a red truck passing makes so much noise.

"What shall we play today?" he asks.

"How about cowboys?" That's my favorite game, but sometimes he only wants to play his own game.

He slaps his pants and finds his gun and says, "O.K.," and then, "I'm Roy Rogers."

"He's dead," I say grazing him with my hip as I sidestep to avoid a pile of dog shit near the corner. "Be someone alive!"

"I'm Roy Rogers!" he repeats emphatically. Michael is several years older than I am, obviously, and he likes to show off things I couldn't possibly know. He is a great fan of forgotten masters of the old B-flicks, like William Witney, a director of the old Roy Rogers' TV films.

Our fight is beginning earlier today.

I give in. "O.K. I'm Clint Eastwood!"

"You're Dale Evans," he says, pulling his gun out of his pants and getting a draw on me, right in front of several NYU students and two old Polish men, sitting on their stoop in sky-blue peekaboo nylon shirts. "You're a cowgirl!"

"No fair!" I cry. "I need to be a cowboy too!"

Despite the gray air and drizzle, there are a lot of people out on the street and I have to keep angling my body so that they don't bump into me.

"You're a cowgirl," Michael insists. "You have to be!"

"I'm gender neutral," I say, wishing I had not left my gun at home, tucked beneath the mauve cushions of our retro modern sofa. Sometimes I tuck it into my panties beneath my long sleek skirt before we go out on walks. And I'd pull it out right now and click its yellow plastic handle and shoot Michael dead. He can be so know-it-all sometimes, childishly wanting his own way. He expects me to be content with our dolls, those ancient steroidal GI Joes that stand in the bookcase, twenty-two of them, and I never want to play with them.

"I'll only play if I can be a cowboy too."

"O.K. Then we won't play today." A slow yawn opens his face. He is covering up a smile. Emotional blackmail! What a prick he is, what a hard-on, what a spoiled brat. "We just won't play today if you won't play right," he says.

"O.K.," I say, stretching, also yawning. But it's no good, because he knows I really do want to play. "I don't care if I play or not. It's not fair that I always have to keep up with you on your terms. It's not fair at all. I never get to go anywhere real with you. We're always riding the range and protecting the camp, and yodeling, and roping the horses, and herding the cows, and playing the guitar, and shooting down Native Americans, and rounding up rustlers, and when we get home all I ever get to do is nurse those lousy dolls!"

"Action figures." He shrugs. We're standing, waiting for the light to change, watching the M1 buses pulling up at the corner and letting off all the passengers.

Pressure gathers in my stomach. "Let me be a cowboy," I cry. "Let me have some gender-bending fun. Oh, Michael, think of me as an actual cowboy."

He stands for a long time, scuffing his foot on the curb, looking intently at the traffic light.

"Oh, please, think of me as an actual cowboy too." Big tears gather in my eyes. "Will you, will you?"

"Well—"

"Please!"

"Well—"

"Please!"

"Well—O.K."

My relief is enormous. Two passers-by stop and look at me as the tears rush down my cheeks. Sometimes Michael can be so nice! I rub my fist into the corner of my eye.

"*Bang!*" I turn around fast. "Bang! Bang!" Michael says. "You're dead!"

Michael has gotten the draw on me. He has penetrated me. He has attacked me right in the heart. I stop, almost in the middle of the street. A taxi almost gets me too, screeching its brakes, the driver yelling at me. Michael pulls me to the curb.

"Well, I got you already," he says. "Game's over. Let's go home."

"You only wounded me," I say in a faltering voice. "It's just a superficial shoulder-wound." I am staggering, my hand pressed to my heart.

"Nah," he says, spitting on the sidewalk. "I really got you. You're dead! Let's go home."

"Wounded!" I shout.

"Dead," he repeats.

And I begin crying and crying, a scratching sound that hurts my stomach and grates up through my chest and out my mouth. There are no gritty tears this time, but my eyes sting horribly and inside my head is the kind of a high, thin sound a television makes when it first goes on. And I'm very dizzy.

"Wounded, please, wounded . . . ."

Michael's afraid that I'm making a scene, but I don't think anyone is really paying any attention to me.

"You only wounded me," I whimper.

"Shhhh. Turn down the volume," he hisses.

"Please, please. Oh, please, please, pretty please with sugar on it!"

He's embarrassed. "I'll buy you a Good Humor," he says, stopping before a uniformed man with a cart, who barely glances up at my painfully contorted body. "O.K.?"

"Can it be over already? Oh, please say I'm only wounded, Michael."

"You know you're really dead," he answers, studying the chart of flavors on the cart's side, "but I'll say you're only wounded if you'll shut up."

"You're so fucking mean!" I shout. And for a moment everyone on the sidewalk—businessmen, beggars, housewives, druggies, hip-hoppers, shopkeepers, students, fashion models, dogs and alley cats—all look at Michael.

He pretends not to notice, but I can tell he's uncomfortable. He turns to me and reaches for my shoulder. I back away.

"Are you really wounded?" he asks. "Shall I ride you to a doctor?"

He tries to examine my shoulder and lower, but when his fingers are on me I get dizzy with fright. For one second he and the Good Humor man, and all the people standing watching, dissolve into a series of frenetic horizontal lines, and I hear static in my head, crackling and popping right in my ears. Then I push him back. I fight my way through the damp air, through the people, and run back down the street. Through traffic, across intersections. I reach our building and open the door downstairs. Up the steps and through the high-ceilinged halls, and scrambling for the keys, I get into the apartment where—rushing to the window—I can see Michael running after me.

I know he'll be at the door any minute. Shall I bar it? With what? A chair would slip too easily. I could hurl myself against the door, but it would never work.

It runs through my mind that maybe I should pretend to be dead, so that when he crosses the threshold he'll see me lying there and leave me alone. Or maybe he'll take care of me, cradling me against him, making soft cooing sounds to me.

I do crawl around on my hands and knees for a second, searching for a suitable place to die; but then, just as I hear his footsteps coming quick and stark against the polished marble, I leap from my position and run to the couch, where I snatch my red plastic gun with its yellow trigger from its hiding place.

He opens the door.

I shoot him.

He falls to the ground, eyes rising, and red, shiny blood forms shapely plastic pools on the floor. Then it spreads thin. He doesn't even cry; he just gazes at me, eyelids blinking, his hair hanging over his forehead.

I fall against his chest, on top of him, so that the blood seeps through my dress and over my body, too.

Then I roll over, and we're lying next to each other. I grab at his hand.

We hug, clutching each other.

"Will we ever have children?" I ask.

"Never," he says. And dies.

THE BABY TOOTH

During July a Chicago heat wave pasted Sukey Rand's legs to the chair in the kitchen. Her mother, triangular with pregnancy, heavy-lidded over mounds of potatoes that needed to be peeled, kept Sukey inside the house helping until they locked up the Evanston man who was scattering pieces of little girls into North Side garbage cans that year. "People are so crazy. Unpredictable. You never can tell," Mrs. Rand said. "Take your father. Why is he staying out so late?"

The enormous radio in the living room ran market reports all day and night ("Wheat is high; corn is falling . . . .") This was Mrs. Rand's revenge. She hated the sound of the radio blaring, the rich, fruity voice of the disembodied market announcer, but she wanted to teach her husband a lesson for leaving her alone. Night after night, Walter Rand would come home from spreading The Great Egalitarian Word on street corners and in union halls, his handsome face unbuckled with moral fervor and fatigue, to find the Enemy's singsong rhythms snugly ensconced within his very own walls.

"Why do you listen to this, of all things?" he'd rage, supplicating the ceiling in despair. "Reactionary! Bourgeois!"

"It's soothing," Sukey's mother insisted, in tears. "I like a man's voice talking, and you're never home anymore. I don't listen to the words."

Bang. The top of the radio hit with the flat of his hand, and the static would crack. *Click.* Off went the sound. In the middle of the kitchen the child would stand glum and limp, while Mrs. Rand pulled pajama sleeves onto her so jerkily that an elbow caught where Sukey's shoulder should go. Then she would lead Sukey down a hallway to a bedroom. After that, Sukey would listen to her parents fighting through her closed bedroom door.

Though Mrs. Rand never admitted it, Sukey knew her mother was frightened that summer about the baby she carried. Two years earlier, a just-formed boy had knotted and died inside her womb. So this time, as her belly hardened and swelled, Mrs. Rand decided to defy the Evil Eye by pretending that she wasn't pregnant, by refusing to speak of the unseen life floating beneath her stretched skin, by refusing to make lists of possible baby names. Inside the cedar drawers, tiny clothes had been hidden from view. Against the wall, an unassembled crib was disguised with a drape. All that Mrs. Rand ever said about the baby, "all I ever ask," she insisted, was that Sukey's father give up his long hours away from home.

"You don't know what you're asking, Miriam. You don't understand the principles of these ideals that will change the world. By the time our kids grow up, maybe we can have a free and honest place for people to live."

"You have to be everybody's hero, Walter. Why do you have to impress people you don't even know? Why can't you stay here with me, at home? Sukey and I need you. Be a hero at home."

A talker by profession, a political organizer, he represented the Progressive People's Party and armed himself against her fears and his own with words and slogans—his form of magic. He believed in words more literally, sometimes, than in his very own acts. Bedtime legend on storytelling nights had Sukey's mother falling in love with Walter when she heard his words—yes, a speech he'd made at a political dance the first night she ever saw him, when she'd been transfixed by the dark gap between his front teeth and his bristling good looks. But when Sukey listened to their secrets at night on the other side of the bedroom wall, she thought her mother often sounded angry, while her father kept talking, on and on.

"These phrases you use, are they something you can hold in your arms?"

"Look, birth is natural. It happens all the time, Miriam. In the Soviet Union women do it in the fields. The doctor already told you there's no reason to worry—nothing could go wrong."

"Shhhhhh!" her mother hissed.

The child hunched into her pillow and sucked on her loose front tooth. She too had a secret. She wasn't going to tell her parents about it until after the tooth fell out and she could show it to them in her hand. In her mouth curled the slight salt taste of blood. Below the window passing cars flashed lights against the sky. Since Sukey had discovered the secret tooth a couple of days ago, she touched it about a hundred times an hour, rolling its flat surface with her tongue until a deep-down pleasure spiraled up to fill her mouth.

In the other room, Sukey's father began to snore. What did her father mean when he said that nothing could go wrong? Were they expecting this new baby to die again?

She imagined the little brother she had never seen. He was wrapped in cellophane, fat hands folded on his belly and a lot of ribbons around him like the white chocolate baby packed in a gold box she'd admired in a store window last Easter. Or did her father mean that her mother would have to go away for a long, long time? Very slowly Sukey's expression changed. Something loomed behind her lids that she barely understood, flickering large and then drifting away.

She pressed her tongue against her tooth and fell asleep.

She woke up to find herself looking at a crowded bureau with her mother's pocketbook hanging from a drawer knob near the top, instead of out her own bedroom window. Next to her mounded her mother's belly, covered with a sheet, and her mother's slack, red-lipped face. Sukey had been laid out during the night between Mrs. Rand and her husband on the long wide bed, which was sealed off from the rest of the apartment by opaque French doors.

"She's feeling insecure," her father said.

"Hmphh." A sharp intake of breath.

Her father liked to act as if he could read people's minds, which never failed to make her mother mad.

"She's feeling insecure about the new baby coming. She's afraid she'll be displaced."

"And what about me? What if I feel insecure?"

Walter laid a square hand alongside Sukey's head so that she could see the dark hairs on his arm, swirling over his muscles and ropey veins. He leaned over her and spoke right into her mother's eye, very low.

"But you're an adult."

Walter had heard Sukey crying during the night. He'd carried his daughter to his room to make the boundary between himself and his wife clearer and more concrete, so that his wife's anger could not possibly overflow into his helpless sleep. At the same time he thought his act might dramatize their fleshly bond. He said to himself, though he didn't say it out loud to her: the Future will be born out of who we are now.

He threw open the drapes to let in slats of light through the venetian blinds. Mrs. Rand crooked her arm over her eyes, where it rested lightly on her brow like a puffy slug. She groaned. As if everything he did hurt her. Why he'd slice off his hands before he'd hurt a fly, much less his wife and child.

"Let's give Sukey some orange juice and make her feel better. Would you like that?" He bent his knees and zipped up his pants, taking brisk charge. He brushed his wife's forehead with dry lips. "Don't get up. I'll do it myself.

"You *should* get the orange juice yourself." Sukey's mother propped her head against the wall. "Why do I have to be the one to do everything? You're her favorite. You're never around, so Sukey really thinks you're something great."

"That's a wonderful way to be talking in front of her," he said, winking a gold flecked-eye at Sukey and sitting down between mother and daughter at the foot of the big bed. "Very responsible. Very mature." He felt caught between the two women, the same way he was caught between his political work and his love for his wife with all her clinging and needs. It made him angry. Why was it a man always had to make a choice? "Don't pay attention to your mother," he said. "She's not feeling well today. It's a way women get."

Over breakfast, he winked at Sukey again, this time
across a plate of scrambled eggs. He wiped the edge of his
moustache with his wrist and tilted his head. "I'm going
to prove something to you today," he said to his wife.
"This girl of ours is very smart. I can have a conversation
with her about things I can't talk to you about anymore
because you've changed. I want Sukey to understand a
thing or two about ideals and self-sacrifice. I'm going to
take her on calls with me today—and we're going to have
ourselves one hell of a good time."

The child studied the smiling oval of her father's face. She
loved it when he used words like *hell*; it always struck her as
really funny. Then she shifted her gaze to her mother, who
walked very slowly across the kitchen and clunked the pitch-
er of orange juice down on the table so hard that it spilled.

"What kind of a comparison is that, Walter? What do
you want—for us to fight over you? She's only a child.
How smart do you think a child can be?"

"Oh, pretty smart," her father said, clicking his fork
against his teeth. He pushed himself up from the chair,
wiped his hands on his knees, and started to grin. "You
know she's got good genes. And even if I wanted to I
couldn't grab all the credit for that."

"You certainly couldn't," Mrs. Rand said sourly. She
lowered herself heavily into her chair and started to eat.
The way the sun was coming in the window, one side of her
face was very dark and the other seemed to reflect only the
flat gray of the sky as she chewed.

Walter was a man who needed to be needed. That was
how he grasped his integrity, his worth. He prided himself

on understanding people and ideas. Only, as Sukey's mother once told her, he just couldn't stand to be needed too much. As he dragged Sukey by the hand to meeting halls and factories, urging this one to strike, that one to talk, clapping men in overalls and being clapped hard in return, the child grew red and puffy as a swollen thumb. She followed his words so closely he was afraid she'd stick her head inside his mouth to see what else was going on and he'd choke and have to spit her out. What would he tell her mother when he brought home a child chomped in two? *"Murderer!"* she would yell. *"You've done it again!"*

It wasn't until late in the afternoon that he decided how to use Sukey's worshipful attention, which both flattered and frightened him. He would educate her about "the facts of life," which her mother should have done but hadn't. They stopped on a park bench, and Sukey twisted her narrow shoulders and ducked her head down between her knees. Her braids brushed light runways along the dirt.

"Yeah, I know," she said fiercely when he got to the part about "planting the seed." Although to find out this time that it had not been done with a hoe and a rake did surprise her. "I know," she said, studying tiny ants walking in a rusty file around convulsive bulges in the earth. And then there was the part about the baby floating, not breathing like a person, but connected up and eating through no-color cord, like her Uncle Joe who had died in the hospital, his lashes gray on his loose, speckled skin.

"I know," she said. Even though she didn't. And Walter promised her that soon he'd take her to the museum, where she could see an orange baby curled up inside an invisible plastic woman.

"How come you know so much?" Walter teased, unlacing her shoes and tickling her bare toes. He grabbed at her. "I've got you now! I've really got you now!"

"You don't have me now!"

She shot to her feet, giggling, and flapped her arms like a wild maddened bird. "Let's race!"

There was a dark wet spot on the rug. A half-sewn glare-white dress sat stiff as a shell on the hassock. Jammed into a corner on the kitchen table was a jar of pickles packed in brine, which Mrs. Rand had taken with her everywhere as camouflage, to smash on the ground in case her water bag broke, so she wouldn't be embarrassed in drugstores or on the street. "Everybody doesn't have to know my business," Mrs. Rand said. "Why should they?"

Thank God, she'd said, when the water broke at home. Walter and Sukey took Mrs. Rand in a car to a squat gray building with enormous rough bricks. Inside Sukey took off her shoes and sat, holding her toes, on a flowered couch in a high hall, while her parents walked away from her, through one fat arch and then through another fat arch. Nurses with cupcake frills on their heads and starched bosoms like shelves passed by, and one of them stopped and smiled and pointed to Sukey's feet.

"What are those?"

"Socks," Sukey answered, surprised.

"No." The nurse rapped Sukey's toes with a pen. "*Those.* It doesn't look nice. Take them down."

Walter came back just as Sukey was about to throw herself stiffly on the floor and pretend to be dead. What if nobody ever came to get her again?

"Let's go," Walter said, pushing his potato-colored hat back at an angle so that his face looked long and askew. He ran his fingers up and down over his nose as if he were trying to push it into his face. "Let's go," he said. "I'm going to leave you with Mrs. Yuskewicz this afternoon and come back. Maybe today or tomorrow you'll get a new brother or sister."

"Don't take me to Mrs. Yuskewicz, Daddy. Take care of me yourself."

"Act your age, Sukey," he told her impatiently. But he let her climb up and straddle him piggyback before he made her climb off again and walk to the car.

Her father braided her hair so fast and tight when they got home that her eyes felt stretched. Sukey sat in front of the kitchen window and Walter stood behind her, tugging and dividing her scalp with a thick black comb. He wasn't paying close attention though. He kept leaving strands out and having to start again. It was making him mad.

Sukey curled her head to get a closer look at a pigeon soaking up gray light on the sill below. To teach her a lesson and to make her stay still, he jerked the comb backwards in her hair. She snapped around, her cheekbones flat with surprise. The big comb accidentally landed across her lip.

Without meaning to, Walter had knocked her loose baby tooth with the comb, and it fell, rootless, in her mouth—a small, hard thing, too small and too large at the same time, unconnected and unbelievable. Blood leaked from the empty space. Her gum felt soft, too soft, like something folding outward. As if it were turned inside out, exposing a part of her that she didn't know what to call.

She spit her tooth into her palm.

"Look, Daddy!"

He was in a hurry, on his knees in front of her, pushing her feet into lace-up shoes with no success. He was using plenty of body English but her outside toes persisted in overlapping the leather fronts.

"Look! My tooth!"

"In a second," he said. "I want to get you to Mrs. Yuskewicz's house so I can get back to your mother. She's probably nervous. Turn around. Let me see you," he said, bracing himself against the table and standing, dusting his navy twill legs. Sukey faced him and grinned large, grotesquely, pulling her lip up between her finger and thumb so that he could see the bloody space where the tooth had been. She jutted her jaw.

"Pull up your socks," he said. "I don't want you looking like a rag lady nobody takes care of." His gaze traveled up and stopped; his eyes pinched at the crooked zipper on her skirt. He tugged it straight, then pleated down the collar of her blouse and flipped her braids onto her back.

"What happened to you?" he said suddenly, squinting. "What's the matter with your mouth? Why are you bleeding?"

Sukey thrust her clenched fist up at him and opened it around the hard incisor, which gleamed small, white, and astonishing, with a tail of red against her blotchy palm.

"Look, Daddy," she said. "You knocked out my tooth."

"What are you talking about?" Walter shook his head. "How did that happen?"

"When I turned my head and you hit me with the comb, you knocked out my tooth . . . ."

It had been loose anyway. She was about to tell him. She had been saving it for a surprise. The loose baby tooth had been twisting itself free for a very long time.

He interrupted her sharply. "I didn't hit you with the comb. What are you talking about?"

Her face suddenly swamped with outrage. He was telling a lie. She searched underneath his flat eyes for the other winking eyes, for the tucked away joke. But his face was stiff and ignoring. He stuck one hand into his pocket and shook out change for the streetcar, bracing the other hand on the bone of his tall hip. The hand full of change shook until he clenched it shut.

"Yes, you did, Daddy. You hurt me." The air in the kitchen didn't move. Only the blue clock on the wall whirred and whirred. He was pretending not to hear.

It scared her.

The shivering began without Sukey's consciously willing it. She didn't know how it began. The trapped daylight heat swelled slowly and angrily into her face, and then, all at once, it folded back into the thin cold of a daylight moon and made her shake. Maybe she was just imitating her father's hand. Maybe it was a trick, like burping up air. She stiffened her muscles tight to stop it— "Cut that out *immediately!*" her father said—but something inside her was sprung and crazy and wouldn't obey. The more she squeezed inside her skin, the more she jumped beneath it.

"Stop that!" her father said. Two veins on his high forehead flushed a purple wedge. "Stop that right this second. I'm going to take you to Mrs. Yuskewicz's house right now."

Sukey didn't want to go. She didn't want to leave her father, and she hated Mrs. Yuskewicz. Why couldn't she stay with her father and talk to him about the kinds of things he said her mother didn't understand? Mrs. Yuskewicz had three powdered folds of chin. She looked like hot pastry, but she smelled like a sardine. She once made Sukey eat lunch under a low table with a fat retriever dog as punishment for spilling milk.

"Daddy!"

Why couldn't her father bend down and stick his eye
inside her mouth to look at the pit in her gum or pick
Sukey up and hold her on his lap? She extended the tiny
tooth like a talisman, already slightly gray and brown and
prehistoric-looking from being squeezed in her hand.

"I want to go to the hospital with you," she said, the words
clattering in the air. "I want Mommy to see the tooth."

He pulled her hard by the hand toward the door, so hard
that she tripped into the leftover breakfast still on the table,
half-eaten; a round loaf of bread thudded to the floor and
rocked crazily, lopsided.

"You knocked out my tooth," she said.

"No." He sat down on the stool near the telephone. "No,
I never raised a hand to you. I didn't." He held his face.

"You did," she said. Her body was dancing, delicately
and amazingly, without any effort, lit up and flickering from
a point inside. She let the tremors gather and ripple, wondering what was happening, why she could suddenly shiver
in this new way. Tears dripping into the corners of her lips,
mixing with blood, gummy, unclean. But she didn't feel
sad. Not really. Almost the opposite. It was as if she
looked out through a very white moon. She repeated again,
only because it seemed to have a most astounding effect on
her father, "You knocked my tooth out when you hit me."

He lifted his head. His shirt looked slick, like skin, and
it was sticking to his chest. His teeth, like slabs, bit into his
tongue, which was much bigger, much darker, than Sukey
remembered it.

"Daddy," she said. "You knocked my tooth out. You
knocked my—"

His black perforated shoes hit the floor hard. His hand
smacked flat on the curve of her jaw. The jolt made her

head fly backwards and strike the sink. She looped her arm over it, hanging onto the wire dish rack.

"Just stop that goddamned lying," he said. "I never laid a finger on you. I never even touched you. Just get up and stop crying, and never open your mouth like that to me again."

She stared at him. He was panting and his hair fell onto his forehead in dark spikes.

Her tears stopped. She felt porous, flushed. He watched her, his nostrils winged.

"Get up," he said.

She got up, cautious.

"Come here," he said. "I want to tie your shoe."

She looked down and saw that the lace had come loose. But she hadn't tripped on it, no. She shoved her feet toward him slowly, as if they were stuck inside boxes, barely moving her knees, crunching her head to her chest and angling her body away from his hands. Behind the bone of her head, a high electric wire screeked counterpoint to the low whirring of the clock.

"I'm sorry," he said, in a soft voice. "I didn't mean to hurt you." With a finger gentle and light as a long-legged bug, he touched her hair. She pulled away. "I'm sorry," he said.

Righteousness crushed darkly in her throat and eyes. Her tooth was gone. He ought to be sorry. It had fallen from her fingers down the dark drain of the sink.

He squatted on his heels until their noses almost touched. "Hey," he said, rocking at her waist. "Don't cry. I want to get you cleaned up so that I can go to see your mommy in the hospital. She needs to see people. Don't you care about her? She's very lonely, lying in bed by herself all day."

She sniffed. Her eyes trained on his chin. "My tooth," she said. Her baby tooth was lost and gone, and he hadn't even looked at it or rubbed his thumb over its shape or even treated it respectfully like the big girl she'd become. He wasn't going to get away with it that easily, she decided. And suddenly she remembered her mother's anger at her father, the things her mother said to her father through the bedroom wall.

"Aren't you sorry," she said. "Aren't you sorry, Daddy, that you knocked my baby tooth out?" Maybe if he admitted it, apologized, he could make things all right. Didn't he owe her something now?

His fingers loosened from her skirt band. He stood up, erect, and turned away. She grabbed at his pants.

"Daddy," she said, half-conscious of familiar words, "Just apologize. Just say you're sorry about knocking my tooth out, and everything will be okay."

He was walking fast across the linoleum. She was running to keep up, grabbing at his leg and elbow as if she wanted them to stop dead, independent of the rest. "Just say it, Daddy."

He walked faster and faster. "Daddy—" she said.

He pushed her sharply away and opened the door into the kitchen pantry, a closetlike dark space that housed the refrigerator and all its gas coils. He shut the door between them.

The child looked at the slammed door. Then she flung back her head and screamed. Her throat was a tunnel. Her screams erupted in coughs and lumps and windbursts. Her father was deliberately wedging her away from him with a hard foot against the door. She kicked at the door, hurled at it. She was frightened. She didn't want to be alone. With no one to take care of her she would die.

"Daddy? Daddy?"

Her back slid down the wall to the floor where she sat with straight legs, glaring out, breathing hard. If her father came back, she would forgive him for the tooth. She would get another one. This was only her baby tooth. She would trade anything for her life.

The door opened suddenly. Into her face. Her father stepped out, straight and tall. His top button was loose, and his clothes—good clothes to show her mother how much he cared—looked skinned back and flapping. He didn't say a word to Sukey, though he looked directly at her. He walked past her and went over to the black telephone on the kitchen wall.

He called the hospital and asked to speak with her mother, who took a long time to come on.

"How are you?" he asked. "I won't be able to visit you as early as we planned."

He was silent into the receiver, his back curved away from Sukey, his hand cupping the phone. "Because Sukey is very upset," he finally said, low. "I don't know why. Maybe she needs me more than you do right now. It's pretty tense around here." A silence again. "No, it's not politics, honey. Believe me. I wouldn't do that to you. It's our daughter, ours. You ought to know me better than that . . . Now, listen, honey, don't you get upset. You're an adult. Are you resting okay?"

Outside the window the light underside of the leaves shuddered on top of a tree. He sat motionless, except for twisting the black phone cord around his wrist. "Uh-huh. Uh-huh. No hint of contractions so far?"

Behind him Sukey stood, hopeful, but with an intense constricted face, her entire small body outlined by sun.

"Don't be superstitious," he admonished the telephone. "I'll tell you more when I see you. It's a long story—nothing to worry about. What's the matter with you, do you love to worry? Look, I've got to use my judgment around here." And he talked and talked, teasing, comforting. He made kissing noises into the receiver. He said, "I love you, I promise. I'm not a person to let someone I love down. I'll be there, don't worry."

He hung up and took a deep breath. "Your mother sends her love," he said tonelessly, sounding tired. His fingers were spread wide on the table. He didn't look up.

"I can grow another tooth, Daddy. Don't feel bad."

She sprawled her body against his shoulder. The sun slid behind a cloud, and a deep sudden shadow bisected his spine, showing a rigid prominence of bone.

He got up stiffly, went into the living room, folded up the white dress her mother had been sewing for when her figure came back, and put it in a drawer next to a crinkled bag of hard candy.

"You're not going to the hospital, are you?" Sukey asked with a slow smile. Triumphant. Following him as he gathered up some books and magazines for her mother, bobbing her head. "You're going to stay with me!"

"Yes," he said. "Yes." Still not looking up. "I'm going to stay with you. At least for a while. You can change back to your play clothes if you want. Bring them to me."

Sukey went into the other room and came back with blue jeans and a cowboy shirt draped around her neck. Slowly her father unzipped her skirt and unbuttoned her blouse, helping her into the soft crumpled clothes. The shirt was pulled on inside out. The big cowboy hero on the front looked faded and unfamiliar. His face was blurred; stitched ridges ran across her shoulders and down the sides. But her father didn't seem to notice or to care. She pressed back into her father's lap, resting her nose on his skin, sticking to him in the heat. She wished he, or anyone, could have seen that baby tooth she lost. It had been so shiny and strange. But a fat new tooth would grow in its place. She sighed and took off her shoes, skidding on the kitchen linoleum like ice skates, something that her mother didn't ever allow.

It wasn't until she heard this funny noise, a dry rustling sound she couldn't place, like paper bags being torn open, that she turned and saw Walter, her father, with his lips curled open wide. He was crying, and she saw right past the wet pink opening of his mouth down to the shadows of his throat.

"Why does a man always have to make a choice?" he said. "Why does a person always have to make a choice?"

And this time when the pain jagged up inside, it was the outside world that began to tremble. Everything was quivering, as if she were looking through water. Then she was water too. Wave after wave, rippling and cresting and crashing into shiny splinters before it broke.

WINGING IT

If my husband's impeccable, I'm not. I'm the opposite. Peccable? What does it mean? Sprawling in my deepest arm-chair, legs out, I look it up in the dictionary. Like peck-able? Behaving like a denizen of an old-fashioned chickenyard, a free-range chicken, where hens and nasty roosters deliver sharp beaks to my head? But the modern chicken inhabits crowded chicken factories, incubated and de-beaked, aggression forcibly curbed, leading congested broken-feathered lives like the homeless men with their stumps and crutches rounded up each winter near my apartment building.

My grandfather, who owned a junkyard in McHenry, Illinois scattered corn to chickens behind his house. Wringing their necks and plucking chicken feathers, he offered up chickens for grumpy Sunday repasts while my parents looked pleased with themselves for taking us on "healthy" visits to the country.

"Don't pick at your food," my father nagged me, wishing he'd stayed in the city as I pushed dead chicken around my plate. My mother slapped my hand. The peppy chatter of Paul Harvey on the car radio had excited her. Her eyes looked boiled, bulgy and white.

On the stove, more chicken boiled, scaly legs and yellow claws scrabbling up from the pot. "Look!" my grandmother crooned, her loose-skinned neck the one my own is beginning to resemble, as she ladled rubbery pea-sized yolks for me, a treat. "I saved the unborn chicken eggs for you!"

One snowy Easter in Chicago after a party on the North Side where the children knocked each other off chairs, down steps, and under tables in the mean zeal of an Easter Egg hunt, my sister and I started to cry. I had fallen on my eggs and they cracked. The mothers swished their nylon-ed legs, feigning dismay at the confusion and noise for the sake of the other mothers, rivals and friends, even as they grabbed their children firmly by the shoulders and hissed clues, secret orders, about where their children should look. The mothers had hidden the eggs, they knew where to find them, but we refused to follow our mother's orders. "Ma, we're not cheaters!" we cried, doubting that other mothers could be as sneaky as our own.

Walking home, empty-handed, our sobs puffed clouds of frost. It was March, an early Easter, and we did not have any eggs. But passing the bus stop I heard a cheep-cheep from the trash can and shouted, "Wait!", yanking sideways from my mother until my mitten slid loose in her glove. I dived into the trash, digging out a shoebox stuffed with cellophane grass. Two chicks, weightless miracles, huddled in my hand, two chicks like me and my sister, thrown out to starve and freeze beneath abandoned bus transfers and newspapers under a blanket of bitter rime. Babies like these, sometimes goslings and ducklings, dyed pastel green or pink, clustered in the display cases of the dime store every Easter.

"How can we keep chickens in the city?" my mother yelled.

"You're a sucker," my father laughed, pretending that my mother was the softie instead of him.

"I'm the one who has to clean up after them," my mother complained.

Then my sister solved half the problem by hugging one of the babies to death, to lifeless scrawn, while I was outside in the courtyard playing marbles. I came in and I beat her in the back until she crouched lower and lower under the chair. Her little shoulderblades protruded like wingbones.

Stop! There is no such word as *peccable*! I need a bigger dictionary. This one is abridged.

Just as I thought, my husband says. I never heard anyone use it.

I sit upright, scanning words.

Peccary, yes, I say. A javelina, a wild pig.

A wild pig lurks in the corners of our apartment, our messy and cluttered apartment, spiny and fierce. My husband is a lot less peccary than I am with his broad shoulders and sturdy jaw. But certain words make you laugh, and peccaries remind me of pessaries (also not listed in this abridged dictionary), although I know from National Geographic they are stones thrust into camel wombs to prevent conception, desert birth control devices, primitive IUD's.

Anyway, I told my husband yesterday when we sat on the bridge overlooking the city across the river that I am not sure I want to have children. For one thing our apartment's too small, our life's too small.

Think it over some more, Sweetie. Don't jump to conclusions, he cautioned. This isn't about the past, it's about the future.

Whose future? I said. I can't conceive the future. Am I a bad woman?

He strokes my hand and answers, Not to me. Definitely not.

Say, whatever happened to the second chicken? he asks me today.

When its comb sprouted, I answer, we sent it to my grandfather in the country.

But was that before or after my mother gave birth to a dead baby boy? I don't know, I'm not sure. My mother never talked about it. She never allowed us to talk about it. ("You have to talk about it, it's not healthy, Jill," my father said. "Of course you're grieving, but you're being silly, you're being superstitious, what about your girls?") We could hear his pleas, her silences, her fears, through the wall. The wall grew spongy. Years later, other new brothers were born and not even my father or my sister or I thought that it was good luck to tell those boys that we had another dead brother before.

How happy and shy we were though, before, sitting on twig rockers on my grandfather's porch with silvery birch leaves whipping below in the valley, my father flushed and stammering, errant dark curls falling over his ears as he explained to us that a new baby was coming. He urged my sister and me, "Press your ears to Ma's belly and listen, listen hard, to the riddle fluttering inside." He belonged to a generation and a cultural circle that longed to be open about the body and its uses; he always carefully left the bathroom door ajar.

"I hear the fluttering," I boasted. Perhaps it was a lie. "It's gurgling like a toilet."

My mother was embarrassed. Her wavy hair, filigrees of gold, blew in the breeze. An artist, she specialized in flowers, not bodies. She didn't like all this attention to inner life.

"And you smell funny. Like swamp water," I told her.

Slats of light fell through the railing. They barred my mother's face. My father said, "Let's choose a name," pretending to consult us when he had already chosen Ricard as the name for a boy ("a man needs a boy"), explaining, "It's a name like our family, nothing fakey or *rich* about it, just a little bit different, not English, not Spanish—"

"Then what kind of a name is it?" I interrupted.

"Like custard!" my sister shrieked. She danced until she fell. She sang, "Ri-*card*, Ri-*card*! I like it too."

"Who is this dead Ri*c*hard we never heard of?" my brothers accused me years later, thrusting a bible at me, my own, purloined, in which during a temporary fit of adolescent longing to have a history and a God I'd recorded the dead baby's name.

My brothers' faces were white, their voices were trembling, as if they'd murdered him.

"Ricard," I corrected, hitting the hard *c*.

There was no murderer. Yet knowledge, putting it into words, a name, made me feel responsible. Our family secret, our silence, implied guilt. But a secret that . . . what? That death had touched us? That it was nobody's fault?

The Sunday my mother came home from the hospital Auntie Bea Ritmanic, a three-chinned neighbor who told me never to listen to my father because he was an atheist and whose oldest daughter Maureen was a nun with periodic amnesia that once caused her to disappear to Las Vegas for three months, took my sister and me to the circus.

There, we stared at wild animals, a leopard dancing in a tiger-skin suit, and an elephant in a zebra-skin coat, a lot of animals wearing other animals' skins, a bear in a tutu, but I dreamed that night of a spindly little blue-eyed baby with chicken wings living in a giant ostrich egg. In the dream the egg was balanced perfectly on top of the majestically high steps of the Chicago Art Institute, where my mother aspired someday for her own paintings to be hung. Then the wind blew and the egg started to roll faster and faster down the steps and before I could stop it, it crashed.

In the morning, my mother sat on the kitchen stool peeling potatoes. When I told her my dream she dropped a long curly potato peeling on the floor and said, "Diana, please pick this up for me."

From the threshold of the braid rug, I watched icicles dripping behind the windowpane.

"Diana, pick up that peeling for me. Put it in that bag."

She turned the potato round and round between her swollen fingers.

"Ma," I said. "The dream scared me. The baby fell out of the egg. I tried, but I couldn't save the baby."

Her lips parted. A fleck of saliva broke from her mouth and flew through the air.

"It never happened," she said. "Don't talk about it, don't tell anyone. Pick up that potato peeling for me."

The potato dropped to the floor. It rolled, lopsided, across the linoleum, picking up twirls of dust. The curved metal slit of the potato peeler on her lap reflected light and filled my eyes. She rose and grabbed me. She shook me hard.

"It hurts me to bend," she wept. "Don't you know, don't you know, that it hurts me to bend?"

So now I'm turning forty and I'm stuck trying to figure out what to do. Improvisation is my natural mode, not dictionaries and definitions, but after that baby died I imagined that other people outside our family knew how to control things that we didn't and I tried to learn their rules. This made me slow. Still, I got expelled from the 7th grade for telling everyone that Mildred Hill (aka Trailer Tush) was having a baby and that she did it in the woods, and I deeply wish that I did not dream so often these days of losing my eyeglasses and my purse.

Perhaps I need more comprehensive references.

My husband, long and luminous, with a premature shock of white hair, angles neatly opposite me on the couch. He is revising an article on the Knights of Columbus, a history professor at Princeton, impeccably genteel in public, with knobby wrists and a playful nature. In private, he is a little worried about me just now, so he gets up to fetch the Oxford English Dictionary, volume 2, and places it carefully upon my thighs.

Between my eyes and the page, I clasp the magnifying glass he hands me. The print is tiny.

Between *pectinated* (comb-like, formed like the teeth of a comb; having straight closely-set divisions like the toes of a grouse), and *peccadillian* (small enormities), I find *peccable*; capability to sin. John Donne, 1631: *"peccabilities, the possibilities of sinning, are the nature of angels."*

Does this confuse you? It does me.

I long for celestial creatures soaring on trumpets instead of the flustered flapping and squawking of my chicken memories, my peccable childhood. I long for an egg, round like the world, solid and unbreakable.

THE TEACHER

Although I'd had several of these students—all graduate art students, many of them as old as me—the previous semester, the class threatened insurrection. Nothing obvious, but constant challenges to my authority. A very smart and sadistic bearded man in the back row raised his hand every time I talked. When I called on him, the first words out of his mouth were, "I don't agree with what you're saying." Then he would cite research sources, often common, sometimes obscure—but much worse for me if they were common than obscure, because I'm supposed to be an expert on the course I'm teaching. I'm supposed to know everything. How else can I explain my qualifications, which should be obvious? A photographer, recently returned to school, working on his M.F.A., this student, whose name is Paul, knows my subject better than I do in ways. Yet his views are too narrow, glinting when you turn them sideways, but invisible and dangerous. He lacks insight. He identifies with the critics. "Look into yourself," I invite him passionately. He's terribly good-looking, but an unremarkable type. And just as he reaches for moral

superiority over me, flipping up his neat fingers to say that
the mistreated prostitute in *Notes From the Underground*
is "the sole character in the whole book to take any positive action, the only *worthwhile* character"—he's not so
infatuated with the Underground Man's curse of con-
sciousness as I am, he accuses me—I suddenly realize that
he is only flirting with me. His attacks are seductions. He
wishes to gain my power. During the class break when I
pass him on the stairs as I'm going down for coffee and he's
coming up, he looks at his gold watch and goes, "Tsk, tsk,
tsk. Late again," shaking his head. Sadism, not scholarship, but for what purpose?

Maybe I'll fall in love with him. I imagine his photo-
graphs, which I've never seen, as fine-grained, detailed,
sharp edges—all landscapes in black and white, overexposed
views from afar. His eyes are light and wide, his hair sandy
and curling. But he still looks ordinary to me, disappoint-
ingly even-featured. His beard, shaved at the sides, is a goat-
ee, old-fashioned and pretentious to my mind; and he looks
like somebody who ought to be wearing a monocle, too.
Instead he wears gold chains around his neck, one skinny,
one thick and braided. Perhaps it's his predictability, the
hand that raises that I'm admiring: "I don't agree . . . ."

At the beginning of the term, another handsome man in
class, and certainly flashier, a silver-haired Australian with
leather wristlets and embroidered boots, argued with me a
lot too—"Not necessarily," he grinned after every interpre-
tation; "Of course not necessarily!" I snapped back—but
his points were silly and poorly researched, and he grew
sheepish when I retaliated, a baby with a need to be looked
at who now sleeps through lectures with his head lolling on
his arm in the front row. A painter.

But most of the students in this class are photographers because of a woman photography major named Tasha—a girl really, she seems to me—who took a graduate course with me last fall and fell in love with it. She recommended my classes to everyone. She's very sweet, tall and thin. Her eyes bulge. Her hair is sandy-colored, like Paul's. Six months ago she wore her hair long and swaying loose to her buttocks. But this year she cut it all off, cropped above her ears. I asked her about that haircut during a coffee break. She said, "Yeah, I broke up with my boyfriend."

"I thought it was a gesture," I told her. "I've done the same thing. I think that when women cut off their long hair, they're often making statements about their identities."

She's intrigued. I'm right. She's thought about it. I've hit the nail on the head. Naturally she wants to hear more. Like who am I? The teacher. But what is the teacher really like? Here's a story about the teacher: the teacher cut off all her long hair into a short burr, a style called "the pixie" back in those days when she turned 13 years old because, although this wasn't in her mind then, the teacher's sister had long dark glamorous wavy hair. I shared a room with my sister. Her hair spread about her on the pillow, rippled over the covers. I pulled my own covers up around me, showing the cropped top of my head, making a lump out of my body. Nobody could tell if I was a boy or a girl. If a rapist came into the room I shared with my sister, right away he'd be attracted to her, never to me. I could disguise myself as a crunch of covers, a pillow, a disarray of comforters, not even a person, I thought then. But I was too large. My sister ground her teeth down at night in her sleep and made tension noises: *uhh, uhhhh, uhh*. Unattractive. But not too often, not every night. I

thought my chances against an intruder were good if I cut
my hair. Yet this is just what I don't want to tell Tasha. Too
personal. A teacher must measure out what to show a student about her own life. One must be personal, but also
self-protective. I'm more revealing, more personal than
most teachers, too personal sometimes, because I'm dying
to get through to them, and I want the students to care
about my subject matter, intensely. In front of the classroom, everybody's looking at you. Or they should be looking. You're too exposed. I'm careful about it. As we stand
in line together in the cafeteria, holding our styrofoam
cups, I say, "Yes, Tasha. I know. I once cut off my hair too
when I broke up with one of my boyfriends." But that's
not the time I'm thinking of, as it happens.

Usually, when a class is difficult, especially graduate students, I rise to confront it. One challenger, one real challenger swinging his gold necklace, like Paul, can wind up a
whole class. What makes you think you know more than I
do? they're wondering. Okay. Disagree! Everyone gets a
kick out of it. Especially when they're adults. It works
well. Competing for insights, inciting each other, playful,
trying to hold on. They have a chance of besting me. Not
a good one. But if at first it only seems about as rewarding
as a dry fuck, more frustration than pleasure and too much
worry about what everyone else is thinking about you,
soon the urgency, the curiosity, takes over, and the questions build. I over-simplify. Of course, the answers are
only temporary.

From the front of the classroom, one can only speculate
about one's students. Who are they? Two very smart photographers are lesbian lovers; I see them walking together
on campus, hips bumping, or lounging under a tree. They
share a studio together and write "uterine" poetry. I'm

making this up, all except the poetry description. I heard
it after class. Another student, Betty Ann Manitou, gather-
ing her notes, heard it too and she giggled, peeking up at
me through the bars of her fingers. But I neither have, nor
want, any way of getting to know them better.

The problem comes after Paul's complaint about me to
the Administration. I don't know why he's complaining
about me. But word slips to me from a junior faculty member at a planning committee. Is it my teaching? Does he
mistake my enthusiasm for weakness, my involvement for
slipshod lecturing? But the class gets wind of it and it
excites them. It excites me too, but with a kind of fear. I
haven't done anything. I'm innocent. Besides, I have
tenure, the Administration can't get rid of me. (Although
I've had to sue to get it, sex discrimination charges.) Now
for them to hurt me I'd really have to act bad, to commit
"moral turpitude," I believe the term is. But I confess: I
don't like to be noticed this way. I'm already called a trou-
blemaker. When I take Paul aside, tugging him surrepti-
tiously from the doorway, the mere act of laying my hand
upon him seems challenging, an assertion of dominance on
my part. "What are you really asking me," he shrugs.
Whatever has passed between Paul and the Dean—a new
Dean, a woman my own age, incidentally—remains a secret
from me.

The news spreads like flames. The students are like
stalled horses, snorting nervously, jostling each other once
they hear. And the class becomes uncontrollable. And too
sudden. At any minute any statement can become volatile,
more than its surfaces. "I don't agree with you." "I don't
agree with you either." "D.H. Lawrence is a Nazi!" "So's
your mother!" Hands wave in disagreement. I laugh it off.
Betty Ann Manitou smiles shyly—or is it slyly?—over bit-

ten fingernails. From the front of the room, standing while everyone else sits, it's hard to tell. But Tasha is the most excited. Or the most disappointed in me. She asks for my phone number to get together for lunch. "As friends, not as teacher and student." But I make excuses to her. Too busy. "Too busy for friendship?" She's scandalized. What is life all about, anyway? She takes Paul aside in the hallway, but I'm not listening to her. "Did you really report her? But why? What did she do that you could officially complain about?" Out of loyalty, I imagine that she's defending me. I can't hear the answer. Only a single word: "Responsibility." Certainly I've prepared hard for this class—and partially in fear of Paul's judgments. Perhaps harder than for any other. Doesn't he realize what I'm trying to give? How much he's gotten from me? And doesn't Tasha? But Tasha's words, her voice, clear, slender and so penetrating that it's almost childish, carries on the dark air down the long hall where I'm bent over pretending to drink at the water fountain. "I don't think it's fair to blame one person for everything. Sure, I had a hard time last year," she's complaining. "But I didn't take it personally. It never occurred to me until this moment that she could be creating problems in my own life."

Paul grumbles an answer, shutting his eyes authoritatively, as if bored. Again I strain to hear while pretending to look elsewhere. But I could tell nothing. His face is clear, decorous, his brow unfurrowed.

There's no reason for me to be troubled. I lie awake at night, looking up at my cracked ceiling, reminding myself that I did nothing wrong. The opposite. I tried too hard. ("Don't like him more than he likes you," my mother warned me when I started dating. *Never too much zeal*, Samuel Butler advises. The same counsel. It applies everywhere.) I feel sorry for poor Tasha, but outraged also. Didn't she recommend my course to everyone? Why did she sign up for two semesters with me if she didn't like it, if she changes her mind so easily? Besides, students love to talk about teachers, to feel oppressed by them. Human nature. Uncontrollable. I picture groups of students in the Dean's office, huddled in deep chairs, dark leather on the far side of a glossy desk, seated too low to be comfortable. "That's your opinion," freshman are always answering. But what's provable? "At least I put up a good fight," I've heard them assuring each other. There's no reason to be frightened, to prepare my defenses early, a series of myoclonic jerks, while I'm supposed to be sleeping.

There are only three of us in the back of the cafeteria on the last day before finals. Me, Tasha, and Paul, all drinking coffee and sitting in the faculty section, in deep armchairs, and they're here because I invited them. They've responded to my overtures. I'm wondering, is it my imagination? Is the trouble in that class some tiny thing I've exaggerated? Paul glances at Tasha questioningly. As if: Should we join her? It occurs to me then that he's shy, he's not aware of his good looks and his intellectual authority, he still feels vulnerable. He needs his self-confidence built up, I've been taking him at face value. Why else would he be surprised that I'm asking him, thinking, *Is it all right? Is it all right?*

I smile gently, trying to confer warmth. Tasha and Paul carry their tall cups clumsily, almost furtively, past a fourth person I didn't notice at first, near the wall, a research assistant to the Dean, someone I barely know socially. I hope she doesn't mind that I've brought students back here; I ask her, tentative. Not at all. When I go to get free refills of coffee, a faculty privilege, Paul volunteers to go

with me. But he doesn't speak about anything serious
except books until we're alone on line, a steel tray rail on
one side and a guard rail on the other, up against the cash
register where the cashier, a mean redhead who always
miscounts your change, has disappeared to another part of
the cafeteria where she's wiping down a steam table.

He turns abruptly. "Don't take it to heart. I enjoy the
class. It makes me think, and it's a kind of discipline that's
very good for me. But I don't like being bossed and being
told what I'm supposed to think, or what an author intended, or what I ought to be experiencing. This is my way of
remedying that, of taking charge and responsibility for my
actions." At no point does he say that I'm a good teacher,
that he recognizes how hard I'm trying, only that he's stim-
ulated himself. But I hear beneath the arrogance, an apology, a plea that passes as an explanation, too humbling to
be spoken publicly, and I'm moved by it enough to reach
out and touch the golden hair on his bare forearm lightly,
an arm of muscular complexity, roped by veins, not pressing him further, an understanding. He knows I understand
him, which is the problem exactly, which is why he's
undertaken to challenge me. The fact that he's in love with
me—if love is what you can call his desperate dissembling
and these disguises—has caused him to report me. More
than fear, it's a purification ritual. Necessary beyond both
of our desiring. He strokes my throat, narrow bones,
curved hollows, and my breastbone, stopping short at the
closed buttons. There's no one else in line, no one waiting
in this cul-de-sac in the cafeteria, but anyone could come in
and see us. We stare at each other deeply. I'm swooning,
clutching at the guard rail secretly, but we stand no closer
in acknowledgment. We know each other well enough to
be parts of each other, we both understand, but words for

expressing it, for speaking and justifying these feelings, aren't available. I don't know what to say to him. I don't want to limit him, I must make sure to give him enough space. To be disrespectful, to disrupt the fragility of his selfhood, that would be devastating. Finally, I can think only of these words: "I wish you wouldn't," and I sway backwards, fumble for loose change, and go away from him because I need to sit down.

He follows me, but he avoids my eyes, balancing his coffee on the plush arm of the stuffed chair. Tasha leans back in her chair with her legs stretched straight, unyielding, in front of her, but slumped, almost to convey that she's too comfortable, looking stuck and surrounded by her chair, as if it has been rising up on her. She rolls her eyes at Paul.

"Did you tell her?"

"Not yet."

"I haven't said anything to her either."

"What?" I grip my cup too tightly and my nail sinks into it so that it springs a leak. Muddy liquid drips onto me. "Tell me what?"

They squint sympathetically at each other. Paul's lips furl forwards confidentially. "Even Tasha doesn't know the full extent. We're concerned about the discomfort in the classroom."

I glance over at the woman I don't know, the Dean's research assistant, embarrassed because I regard this as family business, private, an ongoing relationship, too personal for an outsider to know about. But she pretends not to be listening. Or maybe she isn't, genuinely. A book of poems, bound in red, rests on her knee.

"What discomfort? I'm certainly not uncomfortable, " I lie, for her benefit.

"I'm not either, but everyone else is," Paul says, apparently truthfully, and concerned.

Tasha takes a deep breath. She's arrogated unto herself
a new role: Courageous Truth-Teller. She claims I trained
her that way. "Well, I am. I'm really not happy or comfortable. Something's wrong. And this has happened to
me for two semesters now, both times when I took a course
with you, but I've never been able to get hold of it." She
turns to Paul for approval, rising now with her unmani-
cured hands on her slim hips, light reflecting in her bulgy
sincere eyes and shimmering, iridescing on the burr of her
chopped hair. She makes a demand of him. "Did you really report her to the Administration? If you did this, I think
I might too."

This stuns me. But instead of saying so, of blocking Tasha,
I throw a peek at the woman near the wall who politely
ignores us, then sees me glowering, looks up alarmed, and
turns a page, then another page, of her poetry.

"I think the more individual reports that are made, the
more weight the words carry, usually. But I'd like to know
what you said. You see, I didn't realize that the class was
having such a profound influence on me. When I had a
class with her last semester I thought that I was enjoying it,
the constant pounding at myself, the back-and-forth, the
constant questioning and shaking up ideas I thought I was
sure about already. When my life went wrong, naturally I
thought it was my fault. So many things I believed turned
out to be different from what they appeared to be. But the
truth is, I'm terribly paranoid sometimes, and your idea
never occurred to me. I tend towards omnipotence, I tend
to take too much responsibility, and frankly, I've been having problems all my life. Because I know myself well,
because I'm trying to know myself better, I overcompensate.

I take too much blame. I'm careful not to blame anyone unfairly. Particularly when I like them personally. But if you reported the class to the Administration it might be my duty to do so also. For the record, not for anything specific. But I really wish you could convince me so that I don't feel so guilty about it."

"I wish you wouldn't," I murmur. It seems unfair to push this neurotic, easily influenced girl any further. My role is to reveal, not interfere. To help her come to her own decisions. But how honestly and how very much I mean the few words I say to her. How can this help you? I want to say. Tasha, Tasha. Why did you sign up for my course a second time? Bringing Paul and the other photography students with you, your responsibility, your fault, actually. But I can't defend myself in front of the research assistant. If Tasha has changed her mind, that's her right, my encouragement. I take defection in stride. At least I want it to appear that way. What can you do about human nature?

But Paul refuses to accept Tasha. He springs from the deep chair in fury. "You can't report her! She did nothing to you, you can't report her just because somebody else did! Look, you're making a big mistake. This is the way I do things. Look, I don't let anyone, no matter how much I respect them, have authority over me. I go to a higher authority. That's my way, my reasoning." Obviously he's possessive about it. "My right. But you're sick. You are paranoid, like you said, and you're trying to push off the responsibility for your whole life onto another person. Trust your instincts like I do, but question your reasons for trusting them. Your reasons have nothing to do with my reasons!"

The woman reading poetry looks up from where the book balances on her knee, startled. She stares. So do I. But I, like Paul and like Tasha, am also on my feet now. Paul's defense of me is too strong. He doesn't need to defend me so strenuously against unhappy sexless Tasha. Then I collapse damply with the realization that he is defending me, that he is attacking the poor girl who has revealed herself to him in defense of me. No, don't do it! I want to yell at him. But there is more, there are many more accusations spewing, too many of them. And my weepy sexuality convulses, below any surfaces that would be visible to anybody, thank goodness, deep inside me, unconscionable, and I fall backwards into the faculty armchair, listening, watch, spread-legged. But not before Tasha, unable to defend herself against Paul's vigor and eloquence, starts wailing loudly, at first trying not to cry, then surrendering, hurling herself the length of her stringy arms and body at Paul's knees in a flying wrestling tackle—a leap of faith, I think afterwards, wryly—trying to attack him directly and pull him down instead of crying, but falling at his expensively shod soft leather feet, she falls short instead, with her hands clasping him by the ankles, as if she is grateful to him.

He gazes down at her, interested. "Very gutsy of you," he says, now admiring. But he's not going to stop telling her what he thinks of her, how wrong she is to try to catch up to him. "They're nothing alike, your reasons and my reasons. The two have no similarities to speak of. Yours aren't even legitimate or thought through." By this time he's repeating himself however, his voice grows louder, then louder still, and he's making it impossible for anybody to continue reading poetry. The research assistant sets her shoulders straight and leaves, huffily.

"Stop it, Paul," I say to him. Only once. I can't help him
and I'm afraid of sounding beggarish. I shouldn't commit
myself by talking to him in a commanding tone out loud.
He wouldn't want anyone to know that I have that power
over him. He denies my power. He calls it a killing power,
and I'm afraid that's because it might make him kill me in
order to deny it. Nor do I want anyone else to know I
have that power over him. But what about Tasha, lying
there on the floor? So I give him signals, what he ought to
be doing, in sign language.

"You are paranoid, and you are weak! Don't go blaming
it on anyone besides yourself," he's saying to Tasha.

CUT! CUT! CUT! CUT! I'm giving him signals from
show business, as if he's on the air. I slash my index finger
across my throat to show him that he ought to stop it.

He doesn't stop though, despite my frantic, monotonous,
unending signals to do so. He continues to degrade Tasha,
who sprawls, limp, powerless and despairing, flat on her
back now, staring wide-eyed at the ceiling covered by
square white sound-absorbent tiles.

But why doesn't he stop it? I catch his eye. A brief head
shake. He laughs at my intensity. But at the same time, his
eyetooth flashes ambivalently and he seems to grow uneasy.
When I look down at myself, at the front of my blouse
which he hasn't even dared to unbutton, I realize why.
Little drops of blood are splashing on me. My slashing the
long nail of my index finger, my silent signalling, has
grown too sharp, too frenzied. I've been sawing at my own
throat, a narrow scratch actually, but I have an irrational
fear of gurgling blood when I try to speak about it, and I
find it humiliating, as embarrassing as when I was in junior
high school science class and started menstruating unexpectedly, my first time, blood leaking uncontrollably into

the desk seat and onto the floor, until the teacher sent someone to the art supply room for a huge fold of newsprint to wrap around me.

I rush off to the bathroom to clean up, and worry about how serious it is, have I wounded myself badly? From inside the closed stalls, someone flushes. I run water hard to drown out the snuffling noises I'm making. Outside, through the enormous open windows, pigeons are nesting in cornices or strutting the sill, little eyes glittering rustily, watching from one side of their tiny tilted heads, then the other, incurious. No depth, no dimension, no convergence of points of view with these birds. Their vision is strictly monocular, reality all the way. They're fascinated by movement, and that's all these shimmering gray birds can see of me. A student washes her hands and leaves, oblivious to the pink water. On the other side of the window, the day is warm. Summer is starting. Finals tomorrow. If only I can clean up, it will soon be over. What then? Will Paul and I run away together, or will his hard pride get the better of us?

BROKEN WINDOWS

I've always liked to travel, sampling other people's lives, but when I sampled Eric in graduate school years ago, long before we married other people, I never dreamed that someday we'd be traveling to Mexico together on this whirlwind trip to his wife's hideway on a Baja beach.

Just friends, of course. I told him so. I'd made a deal with myself before I left New York. I could only leave my husband for a vacation if I didn't sleep with anyone else.

But what was Eric's deal? Typically, he didn't say. Eric was opaque, deliberately concealed in spiffy linens, carefully coordinated olives and pale greens, and he wore funny little woven Italian shoes. But I spent a childhood studying people like him, staring out my apartment window into other people's windows, watching what they were doing, trying to figure out who they were. My parents were never home. My mother illustrated medical books, my father, a professional bohemian, was out all day doing God knows what. Maybe the neighbors felt sorry for me. They rarely pulled the blinds.

Or maybe they wanted me to spy on them. It made them feel important. Now, driving down the highway past the flesh-colored California hills, I suspected Eric wanted me to spy on him too. He was a dark window.

"How far?"

"Not far."

My vow of summer chastity, like fasting, had aroused me and sharpened my senses. I loved being with Eric, a happy part of my past. And on a more primitive level, although I didn't like admitting it, I was proud of getting Eric away from Meredith this weekend, too. Meredith was Eric's wife, "an international design celebrity" who actually referred to herself that way, a tiny woman with a Hollywood sense of exaggeration and a tinkling well-practiced laugh.

Not that getting Eric away from Meredith was any big thing. Nothing to go giddy over. Eric didn't sleep with Meredith anyway, I'd heard. Or at least Laurie, my friend in L.A. who worked in their Design office said that was the general buzz around the water cooler about the tension between them.

It made sense. "I believe it," I told Laurie.

Eric never liked nitty-gritty sex that much. His idea of a sex fantasy was like a Brancusi sculpture, streamlined and spacious, uncluttered; clean. But for some reason Eric's streamlined fantasies excited me. I even appropriated them as my own. I used to slip over the surface of him when we made love, sliding fast. His surface was cool and smooth and light. His hands were subtle and severe and sparkling.

Now Eric lifted his eyes off the road and smiled. His warm, quiet attention on me was like a slash of sunlight through glass. I extended my body towards him and the hair prickled on my arms. He said, "You haven't changed much in thirteen years."

"You haven't changed either." I was flattered, not annoyed, by this lie.

I remembered his reserve as alluring and mysterious when we were young. I hoped he hadn't gotten trapped behind it.

We passed through Customs, and a mosaic of broken beer bottles littered the roadside, glass and plastic dumped down hills topped by tin-roofed shanties. Patches of colorful laundry streamed, and in gullies I spotted abandoned tires, dogs with incised ribs and children romping through garbage.

Was it really his qualities that attracted me, or his sparkling blankness that I could fill in? A knot of longing wriggled free inside me, and the feeling spread out and loosened my limbs.

Sunlight shifted over the handsome symmetry of his brow and jaw. I recalled how he sobbed when we broke up, scaring me because it was the one time I saw he needed me. His need gave me powers I didn't want back then.

"This is our little American compound." We'd veered off the highway onto a dusty cliff road nearer the beach. Eric parked the car by an oak-slabbed door in a whitewashed wall. The high wall was topped by broken glass, jagged bottle shards set into concrete, decorative and menacing, and surrounded by bougainvilleas that hung deceptively over graceful arches and red-tiled roofs.

He pulled a bank of keys attached to a pine panel from under the car seat. "Oh, hell! I told Meredith to label the keys. I can never remember which key fits what."

He jammed key after key into the lock. Finally he found the right one and the front gate swung open. We passed into a garden with dry fountains and stern square-mouthed statues flanked by cactus with blood-red blooms. Seven or eight houses, each enclosed by its own interior walls and separate gates, were staggered on the beach slope, surrounded by the outside wall that ran along the road and dipped halfway down the cliff to the beach.

At the second gate, Eric cursed Meredith again for forgetting the labels. I thought it certainly was suspicious, even insulting to me, that Meredith hadn't displayed the slightest bit of jealousy that Eric was taking me here for the weekend. Instead, batting her furry false lashes behind Jean Paul Gaultier half-rims, she had apologized for not accompanying us, saying she had to visit some architectural sites—and practically packed us off together. Was Meredith so sure about Eric, that she believed nothing sexual could go on?

"Help me out. Hold this steady while I push."

Eric shoved his shoulder, and his face turned red. He led me almost triumphantly down the steps to a house, sheathed in glass. It sprawled against high spikes of agave that framed ocean below and the sun setting upon the waves. Gulls drifted on air currents. There were swathes of horseshoe beach and pliant sands.

"Oh, it's beautiful!" I whirled, delighted, pulling back from the view of the sea.

Something stabbed my toe. I looked up and jags of light glinted into my eyes. Broken glass from the top of the wall. Then I lifted my sandal and saw that I had been stepping upon a piece of clear glass that left little white scribbles on the cement. A bead of blood appeared. I bent to examine it.

I saw more glass. "Eric! Look!"

"What? Hold on for a minute. I'll get you a bandaid. I've got to unlock the door first."

"No, I mean look, right there next to the door—there's a broken window. Someone's broken in!"

"What are you talking about? Son of a bitch!"

Iron bars on the low slit window by the front door were wrenched out of alignment and a terra cotta brick, hurled through the glass, lay amidst shards on the kitchen floor.

"Let me see if I can reach the deadbolt."

He rushed through the house. The house was long and narrow with sliding glass walls, terminating in a dark-beamed bedroom on one end and a kitchen with dungeon-like slits on the other.

His breath expelled with a relieved pop. Relief made him happy and excited. "Nobody's hiding. Nobody even got in."

He wrapped a bandaid around my toe.

There was a knock at the door, and we jumped. The crown of his head struck my jaw because I was leaning towards him. My teeth hit my lip.

A muscular blonde with a Dutch-boy bob and a furled face crowded the doorframe. She was about my age, clutching a dingy yellow dog with a very long muzzle.

"Eric, I'm so glad you got here. As soon as I came down from my place this morning to take Ralphie for his walk on the beach I saw the broken window. I drove right over to Oscar down at the *groceria*, and he'll be here to fix the glass within the hour."

"You're great, B.J." Eric hugged the woman, one-armed, looking boyish and awkward. The woman was dressed in drip-dry surgical greens. "B.J. is an anesthesiologist from San Diego, a good pal, our compound protector, as you can see."

"You mean I'm the only one lucky enough to have a schedule that lets me get down here during the week."

"Anna is an old college friend of mine, visiting from New York."

"So I heard." She spoke to me sharply. "Your lip is bleeding."

I touched my lip with my tongue.

"Did Meredith tell you I said to be on the lookout? You know who it was who tried to get in, don't you?"

"Of course. Crazy Sarita. The same one who keeps trying to get in all the time." I must have looked puzzled. "There's this crazy Mexican woman," he told me, "who's been trying to break into homes in this compound for the past year, and B.J.'s the only person who ever catches her. Security's the biggest problem here. We have to work to keep the intruders out."

"Not that I can stop her," B.J. sighed. "No matter how many times I catch her. I'm the one who catches her because I'm the one who's here most often—"

"Nothing stops her," Eric interrupted, handing me a napkin to dab my lip. His voice grew light and animated. He liked discussing the thwarted break-ins. "I don't know what she wants. She eats our food and drinks our liquor and even sleeps here if she can get away with it."

"But what about the outside walls?" I pictured a sinewy woman climbing over the glass and scooping her kneecap like a melon.

"Crazy's Sarita's Mexican." B.J. waved her hand. "She knows the terrain."

Eric hummed to himself and unpacked the groceries, opening and closing the refrigerator. Then he checked to make sure Crazy Sarita hadn't stolen the television, earlier forgotten because it was hidden under the coffee table cube. He joked to B.J., "They say Crazy Sarita's a witch.

Maybe she flies over walls." He returned to the kitchen and began rattling mineral water ice cubes for drinks.

"Could be." B.J. laughed softly and jittered her dog up to her face until his long muzzle touched hers. The dog licked her, and B.J. pretended that the dog, Ralphie, was talking to her. "Ralphie says he doesn't like this kind of excitement. Ralphie says whenever we come to Baja to relax we shouldn't have to worry so much about a crazy *Mexicana* breaking in."

"Or a not-so-crazy *Mexicana*," I answered, thinking of the tin-roofed shanties without electricity we'd passed on our way here. "If I lived with no water or anything I'd want to break into gringo luxury for a little while too."

"Not crazy?" B.J. snapped. She dropped Ralphie hard. The dog thumped on the tiles. He yelped and his nails clicked. "Try telling that to poor old Susanna who came to clean my house two weeks ago and found Crazy Sarita in my bathtub leafing through magazines. She scared poor Susanna half to death. How would you like to come home and find someone sleeping in your bed?"

"Like the Three Bears," I murmured.

B.J. scowled contemptuously. It was clear that B.J. disliked me for being here with Eric—which was odd since she'd talked to Meredith and Meredith herself didn't seem to mind. Could Eric be engaged in some strange *menage à trois?* It occurred to me that everyone I'd ever met named M.J. or B.J. was gay.

"I'll tell you another thing," B.J. said. "If I spot Crazy Sarita again she'd better watch out because I'm going to shoot her. I don't want her hurting somebody."

"You're kidding!" I said.

"I have a shotgun and I know how to use it."

"She's kidding," Eric said.

B.J. whipped her head, and said, "Nope." Outside, the sand blew in undulant waves across the terrace. B.J. stood in front of the enormous glass windows overlooking the ocean. With the low sun shining through her drip-dries, the outline of breasts and muscular belly was visible. It was a massive convex construction that rippled as she repeated, "No, I'm not kidding. Tell them, Ralphie. I certainly am not."

"Creepy," I whispered, after B.J. left.

Eric shut the kitchen door. He trailed his finger teasingly down my neck. "Nothing to worry about though."

He thought that I was talking about Crazy Sarita.

I said, "I mean B.J."

He straightened up and looked surprised.

After B.J. left, other Americans stopped by, audible first, with much clanking of keys and padlocks and laughter, then pressing their faces against the glass, clutching bottles of beer and Cuervo gold and bowls of salsa, beckoning us to accompany them.

"Can't we just be alone?"

"That would be rude." Eric urged me up a circular path to B.J.'s, directly overlooking his terrace where a dozen Americans with comic-strip names like April and Buzz and Jughead and Sundae were lounging in B.J.'s living-room on pigskin furniture, eating chicken-stuffed tortillas, and chattering with excitement about how Crazy Sarita had broken in again.

"Remember, Eric, the time she broke the back window and molded a sand dummy onto your bed?"

"And there was the time she scattered cactus on the floor."

"You seem to be her special love, Eric."

Eric laughed. "Well, B.J.'s had run-ins with her too."

Somebody put on music. April and Buzz started dancing
and, across the room, B.J. made writhing movements with
her head and shoulders. It looked to me like she was loosening a muscle cramp from moving furniture, the kind I get
when I sporadically work out. Then her yellow dog began
barking jealously, and I realized it was a come-hither to
Eric. She was a brawny woman, hulking, she didn't work
out fitfully for thirty minutes maybe ten times a month to
a TV aerobics program like I did. The bullying swagger
reminded me of a Harley motorcycle rider—though, like
me, she was a little old for that kind of thing. When she
flopped in magisterial exhaustion onto the rocker, she patted her knee for Eric to join her, and he perched on her lap,
and leaned back.

"You and B.J.? You're getting it on with B.J.?" I tried
not to sound as accusing and incredulous as I felt when we
returned to Meredith's and Eric poured the two of us
nightcaps.

"We're just friends now. She wants too much. But B.J.'s
not a bad person."

"What do you mean ' . . . now'?"

"I mean B.J. has a bad temper when she doesn't get her
way. That's why we're just friends."

"Are we 'just friends' too?"

"Sure, don't you want to be? Meredith was never jealous of B.J."

I followed him to the bedroom. In a tall mirror above
the dresser I saw the scab on my lip. Eric opened the clos-

et. He shook out the bedding, and stared at me hard. I
stared back, and he seemed to shudder. He shook out
more bedding and tossed it onto a living-room couch.

"Wait, you're sleeping there?"

"It's a comfortable couch."

What was going on?   Within silent minutes, he fell
asleep.

If Meredith *had* know what she was doing when she gave
me Eric for the weekend—or if she wanted me to take his
mind off B.J.—she'd forgotten to label the right key.

Eric slept and I opened the door and walked down the
steps to the beach. Behind me, through the windows, Eric
looked like a man in a display case. I unlocked the lower
gate, and stuffed the clanky keys under a landing.

The surf rolled silver. The tide was going out, and the
sand was scalloped. Soon I came to a ledge of low rocks
and crept over them, strange spongey rocks, soft with piles
of seaweed and trapped shells. The rocks seemed to
breathe as I walked on them, letting out an eerie hiss.

"Sneaking off, huh?"

A hand brushed me. The surf's roar had obscured the
scrunch of footsteps. I let out a low shriek. Behind me,
Eric was rubbing sleep from his eye.

"Scared you? I woke up and all the lights were on."

"I stuck the keys under the steps by the beach-gate," I
answered defensively.

"That's where B.J. always leaves them too. Let's take
a walk."

"A walk to where?"

"Come on, Anna. I have something to show you."

He tugged at my arm and yanked me onto the packed sand.

The moon was peaking, full and bright. I shut my eyes. Water laced my ankles. I cracked my eyelids. Waves curled and I imagined fish swimming in backlit breakers.

"Where are we going?"

"It's a surprise."

We came to a sharp curve. Sand disappeared into a steep jut of rocks. Eric helped me to find sure footing on them. I clung to him.

The rocks were slippery and sharp. At the summit I leaned up and kissed him. I unfolded my mouth into his and pressed his bare back and shoulders beneath his shirt. A faint sweet sheen glossed his back. He pulled me forward and guided me onto a vast expanse of beach with luminous sands on the other side.

"Look!" He clasped my neck hard. His voice was no longer light, but rapt and sensual.

I turned away from the water.

"Look over there, over there, next to the cliff."

A tangle of car chassis and rusting bodies, maybe a dozen or more, lay streamlined in the moonlight like skeletons, naked carcasses gleaming, stripped of hoods and chrome. Above, the road twisted sharply. A sudden turnaround where drivers unfamiliar with the cliff must have crashed through the flimsy barriers and sailed into the air.

"These are car wrecks! You brought me all the way down to Baja, to this beautiful beach, to see some car wrecks?"

"Shhhh! Don't think of it like that." His thumb rubbed me like an eraser. "These aren't wrecked cars, they're stolen. This is a hot car dumping ground, where local kids push them onto the beach to strip them for parts. I thought you of all people," he whispered, "would appreciate this.

The streamlined quality. The way stripped metal just rises
up out of sand. Like sculpture," he said.

"Like sculpture?" I felt confused. The entire beach,
cliffs against sky, rocks against sand, even I, myself, was
frozen and sculptured.

He cupped my breasts and pressed me down.

I felt his tight jerk of attention and looked over my shoulder and caught the silent scuttle of activity between the cars.
Like sand crabs, practically invisible, protectively camou-
flaged by darting movement and drab clothes, I saw a man.
No, some boys—no, no, several boys—it was impossible to
tell how many or how old because they were hunched crab-
like in the shadows, although every now and then one dart-
ed forwards, picking and plucking inside a car.

"Eric!" I grabbed his shoulder. "There are some other
people here. A lot of them. They're watching us."

"Shhh! Keep your voice down, don't scare them. It's
okay, they don't mind as long as you don't bother them.
Act as if we don't know they're here . . . ."

"But they do know. See, they're looking." I braced up
on an elbow. The moon was bright, like a streetlight. His
eyes were bright, like glass.

He pinned me sideways. "Wait a minute, calm down.
Don't be skittish. These are nice kids. They're only the
scavengers, they're not thieves. The good parts of the cars
have been taken already. Don't think of them as thieves.
We can watch them right back if you want to. Do you?
This is the kind of real life you don't get any hint of inside
the compound."

"You knew these boys could see us?" I said. That was
why he had brought me here. "I think it's horrible the way
you lock the Mexicans out. It's their country, not yours,
and now you want them to watch."

"They're just kids, harmless kids. You don't know what you're talking about. They get a kick out of it, they live on the beach. I didn't really plan it, you're the one who came out onto the beach tonight—"

I jumped up, insides wobbly, my blouse unbuttoned, ready to run.

"Okay, if you really don't want to—" Eric pulled crumpled bills out of his pocket, wrapping them around coins to weight them in a practiced maneuver. "I never force anyone, you know." He tossed the bills onto the sand. Obviously he had done it before. The boys fidgeted below, then clamored forward. "But I thought you'd like it. I know you'd like it, in fact. To be watched. To be broken into in front of people. I wanted you to see what I need. Even Meredith thought you'd like it."

The moon disappeared behind a cloud bank.

I ran as fast as I could, losing my footing once on the rocks before I reached the beach gate ahead of him. I scrambled for the keys where I had left them under the landing, and when I couldn't find them, I started digging for them in the sand. Had they gotten buried somehow? Frantically, I banged the lock.

"Don't worry about it," Eric panted. He took off his shoes and dumped out sand. His feet were long and angular. "B.J. probably came back from walking Ralphie and took them. She knows my schedule. She probably took the keys just to be safe."

"Safe from what?"

"From Crazy Sarita. Wait here! I'll run down to Jughead and Sundae's and get up that way. Then I'll let you in."

"No!" I shouted. Sand clasped my ankles. He was already gone. The wind blew hard.

I grabbed at a scrubby tree and started swinging up the cliff towards the enclosing compound wall not far above me, climbing arm over arm, grasping at rocks and plants.

Overhead, the outside lights flashed on.

"What's Ralphie barking for?" B.J.'s voice shouted over the terrace.

I reached the wall. I remembered B.J.'s threats and her shotgun, and realized if she shot me everybody would believe that she'd mistaken me for Crazy Sarita.

But was there a Crazy Sarita? Maybe there was just me and B.J. I suddenly realized that Crazy Sarita must be B.J. Only B.J. claimed to see the Mexican housebreaker. Like me, B.J. was trying to break in. Maybe she would shoot Eric. I imagined him shattering with all the splendor of a car wreck.

My feet gave way. I let myself fall. I landed with cactus spines in my hands. The click of insects surrounded me, and the throaty clicking of night lizards. The wind blew. It lifted me.

Then Eric's shadow loomed over me. He was opening the beach gate. He said, "Let's go down to the water. I'll clean your wounds."

My wounds were many. His eyes glittered, then reflected me back to myself. Closed windows.

I followed him. His back was luminous. Above, I spotted B.J. in silhouette, prowling the terrace. She raised her gun. Light gleamed. Shards fly.

THE WHITE DUCK

How was she supposed to find time to do anything when she had to carry this screaming baby around? Worse, he didn't even seem to like her, pulling his red ears in anger as she walked back and forth, back and forth. When his screams got too big for the dark holes of her ears, pushing into the pores of her skin, threatening to enlarge entrance places all over her body, even under her clothes, she set the baby in his port-a-bed against the wall, on top of the old-fashioned desk where her research was piled in stacks.

When she came back with a cup of coffee, she couldn't find the baby. She looked on the floor and she looked all over the desk, even behind it, thinking maybe he was lost among the papers. She was well-known by her husband and friends as a pleasant but sloppy housekeeper, very disorganized. She patted and smacked everything she could see, feeling for an unfamiliar lump. She already knew that Galen must have taken him somewhere, picking up the baby while she was in the kitchen, and walking off. It was simply a question of finding her. She sipped her coffee, last night's. The great tragedy of motherhood was that she never had time to play. She said out loud, "The baby's large enough, he's bound to turn up."

Nobody answered. She thought of looking inside the drawers, maybe on top of her unfinished thesis, but she found her daughter with the baby in the bathroom, sitting on the toilet seat with her back to the door, holding the baby, her striped polo pulled up. Galen whirled around when the door opened. Lulu saw the baby clamped to her daughter's flat chest, sucking her nipple.

"I hate this, it's horrible." Galen thrust the baby at her. "You said it would be soft and melting, like a rosebud. It's awful. He wants to suck me into his mouth, like he's try- ing to gobble me down."

"Be careful! Don't drop him on the tiles."

Galen looked stricken. Lulu knew that was because of the fight they'd had before the baby was born, when Lulu, tired of Galen's smart mouth, went after Galen, and Galen crouched, trying to make herself small, crying, "Get away from me with your windmill arms!" She laced Lulu right in the belly. "An accident!" she shouted.

("It's the age, you remember?" Lulu's new husband soothed.)

Galen was old, almost twelve, almost old enough to have a baby herself, like whispers at school, girls she knew, Sharon Walsh who the boys called Whale-Tail and took into the stables, and Audry Odum who was so tiny they said she did it with a needle.

"Did I make the baby sick?"

"What do you think? Of course not."

Secretly Lulu obsessed that the baby was going deaf. He had a cold practically since birth, a bad ear infection. Phlegm ran from him like a mudslide. Four, five times a day Lulu clapped or yelled and dropped heavy objects to

see the baby jump and cry. Other times she sang to him.
Galen's brow knotted like an old lady's. Lulu wished she'd
kept her mouth shut. The last thing the kid needs now—
guilt. Last week Galen had shaved her head. Now she
looked like an old man.

"I hate your hair," Lulu said to Galen. "You're a cross
between a baby and an old geezer."

"I'm starting fresh. I can let my hair grow in any way I
want. I'm going to pretend to people who don't know me
that I'm a boy. Do I look like a boy?"

Lulu shook her head. "No way."

Galen bared her teeth at herself in the mirror. "What do
you think of this for a song title? 'Smashed on the
Highway of Life'?" Galen wanted to be a country-and-
western songwriter. "Or would it be better this way?
'They Found Me Smashed on the Highway of Life'?"

"I don't like songs about drunks or druggies," Lulu said.

"It's about road kills, you know. Skunks and cats with
their guts squashed out, only a person who feels like that
instead. How about 'Squished, Squashed and Flattened on
the Highway of Life'?"

"How about 'Splish-Splash I Was Taking a Bath'," Lulu
said. "Did you ever hear that one?" She jogged the baby
on her shoulder to comfort him. "How old is this person
who feels flattened on the highway? Is she a boy, or is she
a girl?"

Galen turned away. Lulu hummed a Fats Domino tune.
The baby began pulling at his ears. He turned red. Lulu,
frightened, raced into the kitchen and snatched up two pot
lids she left out for emergencies and clanged them together.

The baby screamed.

Lulu pushed her face into the baby's tummy to comfort him now that she'd been comforted by his reaction. He smelled fertile, like watered soil.

"What do I smell like?" Galen asked.

Lulu grabbed Galen and kissed her. "You smell funny," she sniffed.

"Like what? Like men's aftershave? I tried some of Rod's this morning. Or has it worn off?"

Galen smelled rancid. Like old meat, like blood.

A nasal hallucination? "Not men's aftershave," Lulu said.

"Hey, Ma! Stop sniffing. You're using up my air!"

The baby gummed onto Lulu and played with buttons of her blouse. He was so little and perfect. The soft spot on top of his head sucked up and down when he breathed. He wheezed and rattled from the cold. His fingers curled and caressed her breast.

Lulu jogged the baby around the back yard next to the lake. Right up until her last month she'd run three, four miles a day to keep in shape, more before she found out she was pregnant because she'd been training for the marathon. Now the baby constantly needed to be cuddled and jogged, a jumpy, anticipatory baby.

Lulu was swinging the baby on the glider on the front deck when one of the flat-faced Spivey boys walked down the middle of the road with another boy, and he cupped his hands and bullhorned to Galen by the mailbox, "Yo, Galen! How'd you like to take a peek at a great big smoking cigar?"

"Get off my road!" Galen yelled. "I'll have you arrested for trespassing. I'll get my stepfather after you."

Lulu started, surprised. The baby thrashed his arms. Lulu bent over the baby's toes, sucking them like lemon drops, popping them out of her mouth with a fleshy smack. The baby flared his eyes.

"How do you like this for a song title, Ma? 'You Give me Cold Loving at the Old Hot Sheets Motel?' Or would it be better to call it just 'Cold Living'?"

"What do you know about hot sheet motels, anyway? What is this song about?"

"You tell me, you're the one with experience, Ma."

"Watch your mouth," Lulu said. But Lulu smiled.

Lulu watched Galen in the back yard by the lake through her bedroom window, screened from Galen's view by the big peach tree. Silver and gold afternoon light jumped on the water. The day was sunny but shivering. For two weeks now her daughter had been both sulky and cutting her eyes flirtatiously at the bag boys in the supermarket where they went shopping. Galen's hair stubble grew in spiky, almost stylish. Color puddled down her cheeks, her cheeks puddled down her jaw, but Lulu could see the baby fat leaving her daughter, revealing the bones below. Her lips stayed full and pouty. But Galen still played with dolls. She costumed puppets. She hid them, so her friends wouldn't see when they sauntered in with her after school. In seven more weeks school would end for the summer. Lulu would never have freedom then to work on her own career between the baby and Galen.

The weather turned warmer. Lulu and Galen spent after-school afternoons outside by the lake, watching the white ducks. Tall grass grew by the water's edge, shaggy thick grass in matted clumps, moving along with the light and the air, the wind tossing new leaves and blades first green side up, then silvery side. Lulu, cross-legged, watched Galen rise. Galen opened her mouth and the wind gusted right into her body.

"It's so beautiful out here, Ma! So pure. Why don't you stay outside?"

"Shh! The baby's napping. I'm going to take him in. I think maybe I can do some work for awhile. When he's up, he's cranky."

Galen twirled slowly, spreading her arms and legs beneath the clothesline.

"Look! The wind is holding me up. The wind is billowing me like a tree."

"That sounds more like a New England transcendental poet, not a country & western song title."

"Maybe I'll be a poet too. Didn't you used to write poetry?"

Laundry heaped in a dripping canvas basket under the tree. Clothespins bulged out of a side pocket. Galen worked on the line, shaking out baby undershirts and sleepers, while her mother worked on her thesis inside. Then the ducks floated by, sweet and streamlined, effortless on the dappled water, gliding. Galen edged closer down the bank so she could see their orange feet beating madly beneath the surface, working away like crazy, ruining the illusion of ease.

"Galen!" Lulu stuck her head out the screen door. "The sun is going to go in before you get even one line filled. You know the dryer is broken."

"I'm doing it, I'm doing it. It seems like all I do now, day after day. I hate to come home from school."

The ducks swam past Galen again in neat formation. That was the thing about it, the ducks were always so neat, the tame white ones and even the brown-colored wild ones which didn't come around much anymore since Malone Buck and the Spivey twins shot a couple of rounds of buckshot at them. Galen loved the wild ducks, of course, but she loved the white ones even more. The white ones clamored when she fed them, following as she quacked hugely, convincingly, like a duck herself, holding out old bread. The ducks climbed up the slope of lawn, comical on stiff legs, walking the way her mother had waddled before the baby, carrying that stupid belly, too big for her legs.

"Galen!"

"Doing it, I'm doing it," Galen cried. She jammed clothespins down over row after row of tiny soft white baby shirts and baby overalls, matching shoulder to teeny-weeny overlapping shoulder.

The ducks began squawking. Rasping with excitement, splashing competitively. Old spotty-looking Mrs. Shagam fed them around the bend of the lake. Mrs. Shagam stamped down the slope wafting an apron full of home-baked broken-up white bread. "My specialty," she boasted. "Fresh substantial bread, good for people, good for ducks, bearing no resemblance, living or dead, to any plastic white fluff you buy in the store, all chemicals."

"I like white bread better," Galen said. "Lasts longer."

Galen and her best friend, Abby, vied to hold warm loaves of Mrs. Shagam's bread to their cheeks when Mrs.

Shagam brought over fresh loaves though. The warmth,
the yeastiness, made the girls swoon. Galen nose-dived
suddenly into the fresh white softness beneath the crust.
Galen plunged, wadding her mouth, filling up, tearing into
the bread with her teeth, shaking the bread, animal-like,
without hands, and spitting out crumbs. Then she rolled
the remaining pieces into dough balls, dough balls dark
from dirt on her fingers, until little putty-colored curls of
bread lined up on the kitchen counter like bee-bee shots.

That night she fell asleep on the floor of her mother's
bedroom, on the far side of Rod, the baby's father, who
organized training videos for fast-food restaurants and
smelled like fried chicken, her own stomach all swollen and
hard, sloshy too, because she'd had to eat the second bread
to hide it from Rod and her mother. To keep from throwing up she drank glass after glass of water, hoping to weigh
the bread down. She crept in and lay in the dark air, listening to her mother's soft breath, to Rod's staccato snores,
and the baby sleeping wheezily nearby. She pushed her fists
into the hollows of her cheeks to control the sickness.

The ducks sounded crazy. Galen had a clothespin stuck
into her mouth, but she plucked it from between her teeth
and laid it on top of the rolled-up clothes and turned
towards the lake. She expected to spot ducks behind the
hedges, half hidden out of sight where the grass twisted,
high and unmowed.

Lulu flung open the window after a bath. She heard the
duck's commotion too.

At first Lulu had a hard time figuring out what was happening in the middle of the lake—one duck arching its

neck, turning its beak to touch its tail feathers, then diving
under, plummeting below before leaping wildly and clamp-
ing its orange bill onto the neck of another duck, jamming
it like Galen and the clothespins, forcing the first duck to
sink. The first duck whipped its head, fighting to surface,
trying to break free. The other ducks shivered their wings
and floated fast, quacking, beaks turned, heads smooth.

"A duck has gone crazy! Look, it's drowning the other
duck," Galen shouted. "Help, help!"

Lulu wrapped her head in a blue towel. "What's the
matter? Galen, what are you shrieking about? Sound trav-
els on water. Don't you know what's happening?
Everyone all over the lake can hear you."

The wind scattered her voice.

"Killer duck! Killer duck! We have to save the other
ducks. Help, help!"

"Get back in the house." The towel fell off her wet hair
and out the window onto a rosebush and hooked.

Galen grabbed up stones from the driveway. She heaved,
lunging forward. The submerged duck, weakened, quiv-
ered its wings and squawked. The stones missed. The
ducks flapped nervously. The stones scattered in dented
water holes of light, breaking into shimmering circles.

Galen flung herself into the water, running hard. The
soft bottom bubbled up from her feet, brown surface weeds
tangled—dead cane and late spring blossoms, already
crumbled. Galen kicked out fast and clumsy, her jeans,
heavy, stiff, pulling at the crotch, swimming directly at the
ducks, hauling arm over arm.

"Galen? Galen, what are you doing? Come back!"

Lulu ran outside, dragging a duster over her underwear.

Galen didn't twist to look back. She plunged ahead, shrieking threats and splashing. The ducks stretched and flew, landing together at the other end of the lake.

"Help, help!"

"I'm coming to get you!"

Lulu couldn't tell if Galen was in trouble—a cramp, a cottonmouth attack?—but she hadn't believed her own younger brother either when he fell out of a tree, telling him to "Stop crying, act like a man, for heaven's sakes!" although after that he was gimpy for the rest of his life. She dived in after Galen.

The lake was deep. Lulu swam fast. Her daughter swam faster. Galen kicked her feet wildly, but Lulu was long and strong and buoyant. She closed in on Galen, grabbed Galen's foot. Galen started scratching and beating at her, punching the water, beating and chopping at Lulu's encircling arm, collapsing into a dead weight, pulling her down, down.

Lulu gasped. She spit out water. "What are you trying to do, drown me? You get back in the house or I'm going to knock the shit out of you."

Galen sidekicked away. "I hate you, I hate you," she said. "It's because of you we have that stupid baby. Don't you ever want to finish graduate school? What kind of example are you setting for me?"

"I'll show you an example." Lulu hurled herself at Galen. If she could have, she would have hauled Galen home by the hair. "I'll show you two examples."

They fought and cursed and scissored the water together, right into the murky shallows. Mud sucked at their ankles. Mud clumped on their clothes. Lulu's maternity bra flapped open. Galen's shirt tore. "My God, what if Mrs. Shagam is watching?"

"Probably, she is," Galen yelled at her mother.

They reached the bank. Gobbets of lake bottom and strands of grass hung off Lulu. Lulu brushed mud from Galen's forehead. "I'm sorry, sweetheart, baby, my big baby, you ignorant fool, but you can't help the ducks, the ducks are fucking."

"They're not." Galen pulled away from her and started splashing at her mother again. "They're not, they're not, these are the tame ducks, not the wild ones."

"You're really stupid, I feel sorry for you." Lulu laughed, an angry eruption, pulling Galen forwards on the slope. "'Fuck a Duck at the Old Hot Sheets Motel,' how's that for a new song title?"

"It stinks," Galen said.

No laughter. She spat muddy water onto the ground.

"Stupid baby," Galen said. She shivered and held on to herself, trailing green shore scum.

Lulu laughed again. "Yeah, the whole thing is pretty damn stupid. Were you really trying to drown me?"

Galen glared blackly. "Of course not, I almost drowned myself."

"A good thing. I'll always be stronger."

"Not always." Galen's round lids trembled dreamily over her large eyes.

Lulu resisted a sensation of tugging, a rush forward to Galen to protect her in a watery embrace, hugging bones and fierce angles, pressing the child back to her breasts. Instead, she gave Galen a hard smack on the rump. "Go take a bath. What do you think," Lulu said. "In this world of random violence I have nothing better to do than save the life of a duck?"

Galen grinned. "Now maybe there's an idea for a song title."

The wind whipped up again, mingled with insect noises and the spring peepers. Lulu pictured herself forever chasing, holding back, racing forward, heeding, forever rescuing. The sky glinted, sullen and coppery.

"Are you coming, Ma?"

"I am, I am."

Galen took her hand. Lulu slicked back her hair.

They went inside to the baby.

IT DOESN'T HAVE TO BE ME

I didn't want to let him in to begin with.

Lying in my long narrow bed. Covers pulled up around me, skin white and dry, darkness outside my shut-up windows. I hear him pounding at the door and think how much I don't want him inside. My body fits this bed perfectly and I feel very safe, even knowing that the room is trash-littered around me with the shells of yesterday's clothing, empty cigarette packs, dirty glasses and smudged white clock lying askew under the night table.

When we were married, when we both lived here together, he used to complain. To look at the dirt, the unemptied catbox, the dust wedged in the corners—dropping the book he was reading (usually a Christian existentialist, Berdeayev, Marceau, he is a serious man) onto his lap and frowning—"What are you waiting for? Your mother to come and pick up after you? You're a big girl now, you know.")

So I'm not letting him in for anything. Not for complaints, not to be told I should have answered the door immediately, that it was rude—and worse—to ignore him.

I don't want to open up.

So I pull the sheet up under my chin and trace imaginary pictures of animals on the cracked ceiling plaster, humming to myself, deciding how he must look standing out there with hair hanging limp on his damp forehead, cheekbones pointed with frustration, throwing his heavy fists against the red door to my apartment. The one I used to share with him before he left it to me.

"It's me, it's me!" he calls. "Open up!"

He's pretty big. I wonder if he could break down the door. (And then, too, pretty good-looking. That part used to make me proud, especially with my mother who married my ugly father and who used to warn me not to like anybody too much. "Watch out for them," she used to say. "Don't like him more than he likes you, you don't want to get hurt, do you?" But when I married Jake—or he me, depending—it proved he liked me.)

"Let me in!" he cries.

Never.

Not after the throwaway polaroids of naked women seen neck-to-knee on the kitchen table at the end of my European vacation, when I was supposed to try out being independent. ("Sleep with someone else, don't worry about me," he said. "I have all that behind me." *I* ended up sleepless in Paris, in the bed of an impotent man, with a prick the size of my thumb, who carried, jangling in compensation from a belt around his waist, the keys of nineteen women.) Not after he, Jake, kept women in my bed during that vacation, introducing them to my neighbors, my butcher, my fresh fruit and vegetable man. Piling up incense burners and herbs and body oils, presents from them in the hall closet. After he let them wash out my bathtub and my toilet so that they were the cleanest I had ever seen, so that I cried when I saw them because he was so sweet, he missed me so much

that *he had done that*, I thought. Got down on his knees on
the bathroom floor for me.

Never.

I don't hear him anymore. Is it possible he's gone? Well,
I might as well find out.

And I'm out of bed, tripping over a book, bumping my
nose against the kitchen cabinet because of the burnt-out
light—can't see—and silently tiptoeing down the hall. I
reach the door and press my body against it.

I don't hear him.

Testing. I begin scratching at the door a little bit, like an
animal, it could be a rat, it doesn't have to be me. I'm not
committing myself to anything, Jake, you don't know
what's making this noise on the other side of the door. . . .

Nothing.

And then a little louder. Using all my fingers. *Testing.*

"Open up!" His voice, so close, so loud against the door,
shakes the wood and vibrates in my ear, making my hair
ache at the roots and blasting one side of my face. "For
Chrissakes, Amy, let me in!"

"Why?"

"Just open the door, will you? I'm not going to stand out
here and beg. This is a terrible thing for the neighbors to
see, you know. We might as well be a couple of Chinese
immigrants or something."

The neighbors are going to love that. Most of them are
Chinese. But he doesn't give a damn, he grew up in Great
Neck, multiculturalism is an academic term for him, and
that's not who he's thinking of, not real neighbors. No.
For him some kind of cosmic neighbors, something
Christian existential no doubt, the Big Neighbors in the
Sky. The Super-Neighbors who were everywhere, who saw
everything you did, the same ones my mother talked about,

who watched you when you were a little kid and naked in
the bathtub, who got under the covers or used supermanic
X-ray eyes to see when you touched your slitty with your
fingers. Who saw your big fantasies about grown men,
wearing black hats, sitting on each others' shoulder with
ding-dongs touching. Who knew the time you stuck a purple crayon up the baby-hole you didn't know was there and
put the germs inside it. And those crayon germs gave you
twenty years later, a burning yeast infection, leaking out
your underpants and chafing your thighs, for weeks walking around stiff-legged like an inverted V.

Those neighbors.

"You're the one who's making the noise," I said.

"Let me in."

"Let me in," I mimicked, laughing sharply, the door
between us. Yet knowing that I'd open up and it would
only be harder this time. He'd get mad, I'd cry, he'd feel
good, we'd fuck.

Big deal. *Christ, what are patterns for?* Amy Lowell said
that and she was a dyke and smoked a big black cigar.

Why bother?

So I open the door, and he comes in. And for one minute
I have a quickie fantasy that it's not him, it's someone else,
someone unknown coming to woo me. The *landlord*
maybe. G.G. Stern. G.G., who came once for the rent
when I was in my nightgown and leaned in the door wearing a gray fedora and black coat and holding, with prominence, a black book in his hand. With marks next to my
name. (Could it be the Neighbor Book? The one with the
marks about what I'd been doing in secret all these years.)

And he leaned his hand against the door in the darkened hall and then shifted positions and leaned his hand against my breast. Nonchalant. Impersonal. Talking about the hot water situation, not even looking at me, his hand squeezing in and out.

I was talking about the repairs he should make. "Could you please fix the holes in the wall . . . the windows are loose. . . spray the roaches!"

And he was yelling at me, indignant. Taking his hand off my breast and—I think—dusting it off on his gray flannel knees. Pointing out unswept floors, beyond—dishes in the sink. Saying the same things to me as Jake. I had a nerve! For Christ's sakes, he could *report* me. To the Board of Health. And closes his book after marking my name.

But now, with Jake inside the door I think that it could have been different. G.G. could have been coming to rape me knowing that I didn't have a prayer, that no one would believe me against him. And forcing his way in and on me, there on the spangled-dust hall linoleum, and then just as he came, the Transformation. G.G. loving me. As he shot into me like jelly from a tube, Orthogynol Economy Size, until he was flattened out and folded up. And me so soft and beautiful there on the floor underneath him, all covered with dust. A satin-skinned lady. And he carries me into the bathtub and lays me down and turns on the faucet, lathering me with soap from head to toe. All over.

Jake says loudly, "What are you doing? Very funny, I bet you think. Keeping me out there in the hall screaming like a bloody lunatic. Somebody could have called the police on me. You know I don't have a key anymore."

"It never occurred to me."

"What were you doing, jerking off? Didn't you hear me?"

"Women don't *jerk* off, Jake, it's not anatomical." My god, you'd think we were still living together the way he's talking to me.

"What did you mean leaving after one glass of wine like that? You know I was planning to take you to dinner, you know I came without Lisa because I wanted to see you. We have to talk about the business end sometimes. A lot of things need straightening out."

"Yeah, Jake, you want to get something straight between us," I say. It's a line from an old and dirty joke.

"For instance, what about the telephone deposit. I put down two hundred and five dollars on that phone, and I think in all fairness you ought to pay me back. After all, you're still using our name."

"That's pretty cheap."

"I'm not exactly rich, Amy. Artists don't get supported by patrons anymore."

Like I did, he means. By him. The way we lived on his inheritance, eating brown rice until my skin turned the same color. To save money. And because Ohsawa said your shit wouldn't stink if you were healthy and exercised and ate brown rice. Jake thought clean shit was terrific.

"I don't have the money," I say, which is a lie. But is that really all he came here for? A hurt is scratching at me. Poking, until my vision grows soft, as if under water. Jake wavers uncertainly, looking down at his shoes. (The time he gave me a baby rose, surprised by a snow storm, frozen in ice: do you remember?)

"What about the wedding presents," he says. "My brother Paulie gave $250 and so did my great-uncle

Martin. What happened to them? Look, I think it's only fair that we split the money, don't you?"

"That was four years ago," I say. And turn away. Walk down the hall and into the studio bedroom, to hell with the dirt. He follows me, sitting across the room, switching on a lamp, then leans into the carved oak rocking chair we picked out together from Good Will. His pants pull tight across his thighs. His hand resting near his crotch is limp, but I can see his large knotted knuckles.

This is ridiculous. For three years I was married to this man, even if it did take place at City Hall. Promised to love and honor him, even though he was so cheap that on our way there, when a smiling homeless man asked for a quarter he wouldn't give it to him. "It's bad luck, Jake," I told him. So what? "Let him work like everyone else," Jake said. (Except him. His mother died.) And afterwards we went to Chinatown for egg rolls and champagne, some downstairs place we never were before or after. (Did you give me the frozen rose because it was free, Jake?)

Then we hopped a Trailways bus to Maryland to tell my parents and Jake looked so good to my mother that she invited all the neighbors over for a celebration brunch. And all of them, hugging me, told me how lovely, how ecstatic I looked. "Oh, marriage agrees with you!"

But we'd been living together a year-and-a-half. We got married because I started crying everyday. Finally it came out that I thought we should, my parents thought the way I was living was awful. I was twenty-two years old. It looked like we were breaking up, and I ought to get some credit out of this anyway. An honorific. A *Mrs.* A ring that every time I got on the cross-town bus I looked at the other women on the bus, and some of them—my grown-up equals—had rings too. But some didn't and I felt I was in a special womanly class, holding out my finger as if it were arthritic to show it off, and saying "my husband" as often as possible. But the point here is that I certainly didn't look as if marriage improved me. My hips had spread, my eyes sprang tributaries, and my complexion was now brown rice.

"Did you come here just to collect, Jake? Maybe you'd like your security back too."

"There's no point fighting," he says. "We're two reasonable adults."

"Sure. Me and thee." Then I pause, waiting.

"I never said it was your fault you can't handle details. It's not in your make-up, so you don't have to act like I'm insulting you or something. Do you think I like taking part in your paranoia?"

He's plucking my ever-resonant string of self-doubt, playing it to the chorus of disarray around me—my life, my apartment, my bankbook—with great familiarity, an old favorite. He's hoping for my solo, my big number, "I'm sorry," but I'm not giving it to him.

"Just don't expect me to stoop to counting pennies," I say.

"For God's sakes, who asked you? I'll do it myself."

True. He will. One time he swept the floor to teach me a lesson, later with pursed lips shoving $11.87 in dusty change at me. Found under the bed, refrigerator, magazines and shopping bags. "Do you know what this means, Amy? A real macrobiotic—eating #7 brown rice—could live on this money for an entire week. Aren't you ashamed of yourself?"

"Oh, Jake, this is ridiculous.

His lips are shining at me in the 60 watt darkness of the room with no illumination from the burnt-out kitchen.

"Look," he says, "I made up a list. You don't have to get so excited because it's all down here, and—"

"A list?"

Yes, he squints into the lamplight, reading out loud. Itemizing past credits and debits, trying to come to zero. I feel terrible, but a smile begins to quiver off my face. Out of control. At the point where he begins to account for depreciation, offering me a consumer index from his pocket, he looks up at me and frowns.

"Don't you take anything seriously? This is no laughing matter. Amy!"

When it was over, I started to cry. Tears beating me out by an eyeblink and keeping the pattern the same. Undisturbed. We ended up in bed, my body cresting and breaking like an ocean, pulling at him as if I wanted to drown him, sucking him under to the bottom of my being. Beneath the waves a hot hollow ball rises, but a net of feeling anchored below traps it, tangling around, until it just bobs up and down, caught, becoming painful.

Until I don't feel like an ocean at all. More like a kitchen sink. Jake is scraping me, rubbing, brillo-hard, Jake is saying HOT water, HOT water, HOT water, can't you do anything right? He rolls over to sleep, nudging me in the side, and says, "You didn't let yourself come, did you, baby?"

Outside the moon is rising. A crescent, a sliver, above the jagged building tops.

It's still early, although Jake is snoring, spit flecking the side of his mouth like a baby. I touch myself with the tips of my fingers, feeling my rawness. Then I open the window and let the sky come into the room, picking me up. My body rises effortlessly, my hair floats around me. And in the warm darkness I look below at the city, and in front, above me, the lights. Planets. The sickle moon. So I spread my thighs and land on its cool white-gold tip, letting it penetrate me. Rocking back and forth, leaning against its sharpness until it slides, melting, inside me. Then arching my back and wondering what the neighbors would say if they could see me now. Some of them are watching, of course. Lovers, lying out on the roofs of tenements, children playing on the fire escape to get out of their parents' way, poets, people with cricks in their necks. Even G.G. Stern, bored, having nothing to do in his penthouse apartment in Queens, decides to look up at the moon tonight, taking from a black case the expensive telescope he uses and setting it up, unfolding its thickness, pulling it out longer and longer, jiggling the end to improve his focus. He sees me. And satisfied, makes a stream of comments into the Neighbor Book, then rubs his hands over and over on his bald head until I come. Back to my bed and shut the window. The moon sets.

THE COUSINS' CLUB REUNION

I've always loved vacations that somebody else plans, but
In ever expected this reunion that started out with me losing my clothes in a country hotel—misplacing my earrings
and scratching my glasses so that the blurred halo effect
made me doubt my eyes—to turn out this way. Then on
top of everything I discovered that my suitcase was missing.
I would have been convinced that my mother took it by
accident, except that my mother wasn't there, she was
home in Virginia with a bad cold.

Downstairs, my cousin Morton waited in the driveway
patiently in a gray stationwagon full of heaving flesh, relatives squashed onto each others' laps, while I frantically
searched under beds and in drawers, despairing. The problem is, I have no privacy. People keep walking in and out of
these rooms, even though I barely recognize them. A man
and woman in their mid-thirties, look-alikes, married, with
muscular jawlines, fling themselves onto my bed, bickering.

"You're lying on my blouse," I gasp, tugging at them anx-
iously. "Please don't."

The woman smirks bitterly, rolling sideways. "You're so
vain, I'll bet you think this fight is about you . . . ."

"I hope not."

I run into the hallways, examining myself in the long mirror. My outfit, a heavy red sweater with silver threads up the nub, and black tights, twinkles raffishly, perfectly fashionable for this occasion and vaguely sleazy, just the look I want. God, I'm tired of being a good sport, though. But somebody has to take that responsibility! When I return to my room, I undress and pack the clothes in a plastic bag, then realize that I have packed the sweater and tights too and I'm wearing nothing, although it's cold; even my feet are bare. Cousin Morton begins honking the horn.

"Hurry, hurry," Morton yells up through the steamy window, words rising in the cold, crystal clear, rivulets running down the glass, swelling the sash; rotten wood. "Come on, come on, it's almost dark. The mountains are casting shadows. We're missing the sunset."

My tights twist backwards when I pull them up. I start over again. A splinter pierces my foot. But what sunset, I'm thinking. Outside it's dark already, as far as I can see. We're so high up, where can we be going that the sun will still be setting when we get there? Like a late afternoon jet flying to the West Coast following fuchsia clouds. And how fast?

A boat, evidently. A cruiser, anchored in a copper bay. We sit below at long tables, wooden planks like pilgrims must have dined on, and somewhere, on another boat perhaps, a band plays "Unchained Melody," my formerly favorite song. At the same moment, I realize that an aunt who looks exactly like my mother, scimitar nose and slanting eyes, a narrow-strapped gown loose on one shoulder and shrugging down, is waving an eloquent hand across the table at me, discussing sex after sixty with a group of

younger men, again look-alikes, all sizes and shapes, who
are my cousins, naturally.

"Well, I really don't enjoy men that young, they're too
preoccupied, obsessed with themselves." Apparently, she's
arguing with me. "I was with this younger man the other
night who was terribly slow and considerate, but the whole
time he was thinking, *performance! performance! how'm I
doing?* I could tell. Was I assessing him?" She questions
humorously in a rising voice. "Am I the Judge?"

I wondered if my mother was having other affairs too.
Shocking, I thought. Then I thought, probably. She's not
dead.

Tuxedoed waiters bear platters of corned beef, roast beef,
Chicken Kiev, fat-mottled, long curled salamis.

"Look, Aunt Min, here comes Uncle Charlie on a bed of
sauerkraut!"

"Don't be crude!" My aunt swats an adolescent boy who
ducks under the table, rattling silverware down onto his
head to get away.

"Let me see the slides of Cousin Charlie's wedding."

"How we age, oh, how we age!"

Unfortunately, my breast is being fondled by semi-
moronic Cousin Newton, who I don't believe I've ever met
before but find strangely sexy. A Gulf War vet, everybody
cautions me to humor him. His smooth-browed hydro-
cephalic head is up my sweater in no time at all, and he
unhooks my bra.

Aunt Min says, "Isn't it nice to have the Cousins' Club in
a new place?"

We're barely out of port before Newton and I have an
affair that includes his girlfriend Cheryl Maserjian, heavy-
lidded, inscrutable and terribly dumb, dark rings around
her amber-lit eyes, masses of glossy curls, an Armenian yet.

But that she can't be related to me turns me on: no blame. Intellectually, though, I'm not interested in her. Her body tastes like deep clay, gritty and moist, and with my hands, with Newton's hands, we mold her in our own likeness.

"Last year I changed my name to Tree, Cheryl Tree," she informs me personally, drinking Amaretto afterwards. "I wanted to choose myself, to choose my own name."

"Getting back to your roots?" Newton giggles, interrupting. She's heard it before and continues, ignoring Newton.

"But I felt guilt. Armenians barely exist since the Turks massacred us, we've been despised, and I couldn't see denying my heritage. It's bigger than I am. I wanted to be free yet I'm responsible to a culture too. So I figured out a way to do both. I changed my name to Treeserjian, Cheryl Treeserjian, definitely Armenian."

"Treeserjian?"

"People called her to cut and suture their plants—"

"Too horticultural," Cheryl agrees, savoring the word.

"You're smarter than Cheryl," Newton assures me. He climbs up on top of a bench and waves his prick above the food, a hose-like prick that is unplumed at its base, only lightly roseated: Newton is strangely hairless. Gulf War Syndrome? "Do you like me?" he asks. And then, nervous because I don't say right away, he flings his arms out and shouts, "I'm an airplane, I'm an airplane, a bomber, watch out, a B-12! Br-*room*, bbrr-*room!*" Buzzing, he squeezes past people, circling.

Secretly I yearn for Cousin Morton, though, who brought me here. Thick and swarthy, a pharmacist with oily eyes, Morton is impossible, however. A first cousin. Too close. He watches me sardonically. He likes refusal, loves control. I'd be willing to give in. But I'm glad he's firm.   A rock, my strength, he prevents compromise. Morton is immoveable.

"Hi, Morton," I tease from between Cheryl's legs, cheek pressed to Newton's narrow butt, peekaboo, fluttering a few fingers, innocent and friendly.

He turns away, expressionlessly. Very seductive to me. God, I lust for him. In fact, confused, sloe-eyed, sex-drugged, I make a mistake during the salad course, between family jokes and old songs, while Uncle Muttel dances the *kazatske* like a young man and a lean quivering waiter plays the violin; I call Newton *Morton*; I call Cheryl *Morton*. Cheryl spits wine on me. We effervesce together. I'm a good sport, terribly popular, and Cheryl is too. I'm not mad. Besides my sweater's already red. But her feelings are hurt, I know, even as she laughs. To make it up, I send secret acceptance signals, I praise Armenian rugs, mention that Gurdjieff was a secret Armenian, display esoteric knowledge, discuss Armenian drums, spices, and grilled rack of lamb. Cheryl grows drowsy, sullen, anyway. Her head sways, her hips droop. "It's not fair that I can't be a member of your family," she whines. "That's why you're prejudiced against me. I had sex with you, the least you could do is know my name. . . ."

Her stolid honesty touches me. And her swaying hips. True, true. She's not like my family. How little she needs from me, actually.

Morton fondles her ass, contemplative, as she rolls and arches under his big hands. "Over-ripe cantaloupes," he laughs, sending her off with a hollow smack, her flesh jiggling. "Doesn't Aunt Sylvia look like Queen Elizabeth in her green dress in this photograph?"

"Prettier," Aunt Min defends.

"Don't put greasy fingerprints on the celluloid. Hold the edges!"

Sticky with saliva and sweat, and trembling, Cousin Newton and I exchange looks, slide under the table where several older relatives knead and tickle our exposed flesh with their bare toes, or prod gingerly with Murray's-brand space shoes, Mephistos, or pointed patent leather. In my lap, Newton, cradled to my breast like a baby, his long, pale, naked legs hanging down and his toes curled, rubs cheesecake into my nipples and he sucks. The cheesy filling makes squirmy worms, and he rubs and rubs and the worms grow longer, and dirtier, and squigglier. "Graham cracker cr-*rust* . . . !" he grunts, explosively. And my breasts, heavy and unloosed, tipped with mauve, a rogue hair glossy, are now discussed and analyzed by Uncle Leo, Uncle Morrie and Cousin Duane. Older women are more attractive than we're cracked up to be, I'm thinking. "Cracked?" Morton winks, reading my mind. "That's a pun." Morrie spreads chopped liver on wheat thins and intones visions of hungry Amazons astride froth-flanked mares. Aunt Min threatens sea-sickness.

"Oh, oh." Morton taps my thigh. His mouth purses, unamused. "Here they come. Listen, don't you hear their motor? I didn't think they'd have the nerve. The wrong side of the tracks is approaching."

Down the hatch, in single file, dressed in black silk, ceremonial display, parade the rich relatives of our large family, the Mizooks, that family of crooked politicians and ambulance-chasers exposed on the Sally Jesse Show, who have CIA contacts, sell weapons to Libya, throw dinners for the FBI. "At least I know I'm a better person," Aunt Min insists. The baby-faced brains of the outfit, Cousin

Sheldon in a beaver-trimmed hat, flicks his cigar ashes on Cheryl Maserjian's lap.

"Our private dinghy is waiting," Sheldon says.   The dinghy taps our boat's side.   "We want to convey. . . regards."

"Oh, Rosalind, Cousin Rosalind!" Morton sighs. "There's Rosalind," he calls out, but his breath is leaky, as if an undertow has caught him suddenly.

Yes, Rosalind, it's Sheldon's sister fair Rosalind who attended Charles Kozminski grammar school with me and who even as a chunky ten-year old with gold ringlets wore the blasé expression of a dissatisfied matron and snubbed me regularly. Who cares?

Newton is holding my turgid nipple between little teeth, his hairless legs crossing like an up-ended frog. He looks sideways, curious.

"Rosalind! It's me, it's me and Cousin Kadey, it's me!" Morton shouts desperately.

"You were richer but I was smarter!" I shout too. "Remember?   I won I Speak for Democracy in the seventh grade?"

Holding the neckpiece of her black coat, a dark fur, Rosalind's lips round to form the question: "Who? Who?"

But Rosalind has now thinned, her face angled elegantly, horizontal planes and fat lips turned sensual; green eyes, sunlight through a flash of forest canopy, study us carefully. Rosalind is detached.

I plead abruptly, "Rosalind, open your coat!"

Some relatives, like Rosalind, change remarkably. Others literally, happily, remain the same. Yet up close I must admit, Roz has more wrinkles than I do, fine lines, dainty networks extending from her eyes, lacing her cheeks, visible as shadows, pink on white, or blue, a faint loosening of

the lids. Her hand, pearly, opalescent, from another view
looks lizardy. But folds of wool that she refuses to part
can't disguise the heady smell of turpentine wafting from
between her breasts and oil of linseed pulsing at the tem-
ples. Flaxen hair curls moistly on a fair brow. She glows,
phosphorescent; zinc white, cerulean blue, line her fingernails, and spatters of cerise. Roz is a painter. In the *New
York Times* I've seen her name. Rosalind, Rosalind, how
I yearn . . . .

To take a shot in the dark: "Too bad your life has turned
out miserable."

Rosalind begins to cry. Morton, heavy-hipped with sor-
row, a sunken man, lumbers after her, shaking his fist back
at me. "Why do you want to hurt her?"

"Let me back on your lap," Newton calls up to me from
the floor. I hold his downy head and let him clamber higher, but I'm angry at him for deserting me in my time of
need. I'd begged Newton to help. "Newton," I'd implored,
"Newton, shield me with your long body, shield me from
comparison with Rosalind, I don't want her to see me
before I see her. Please, Newton, please, it's important to
me. Please, please."

"Why?" Newton grows playful, flirtatious between
splayed fingers like a baby.

"I'm shy," I stammer.

"You're shy?" Newton guffaws. "Like heck," disbelievingly.

"I may not seem shy, but I am. Believe me." Urgently
trying to convince him, pulling him by the armpits up in
front of my face so that only my dark eyes, floating dark
hair and arching browline, expressive, my best features, are
visible over his sharp bones, light musculature. He holds
back. So furious am I then at his stupidity that I dig my
nails in to hold him up until he screams, yanking higher,

higher, like a big mask. "Newton? I'm sorry. I apologize. Please, Newton, stay still. Just for a minute Newton. Please, please!"

Newton falls off my lap.

"Newton, you're so *sallow*, are you sure you're well?" Rosalind cries then, running backwards, concerned, Morton panting and turning to slew after her like a tame bear.

If only Newton or Cousin Morton would be more protective of me! How come I always have to take care of myself?

Below, in the pit, rowdy laughter and gasoline fumes rise over the roar of engines. But somebody is calling my name. I push Newton aside, under a table with my foot to get a better peek, and Newton drops over compliantly, pretending to be dead.

"John Downey!" I shout, incredulous, recognizing below the witty unflappable Irishman I used to work with, a writer too, all togged out in a tuxedo with a whole group of happy men in tuxedos, another party, with toasts and songs, and I slide down a pole to reach him. Years ago John Downey lived under shaking crystal chandeliers in a studio apartment in Brooklyn Heights, sharing his bed, next to a refrigerator, with his faithless wife Dierdre and occasional lovers. And their refrigerator, back then, instead of itself, was a gigantic bookcase, each wire shelf sagging with important works. Even their table and the double bed were the same furniture item to save space. No, I'm wrong. Their table was a bathtub. A bathtub with a tin lid. Long ago, John Downey moved away when he divorced Dierdre and lost his job. Gosh, I'm happy to see him now.

Although he's yelling and catcalling, a little too casually, trying to impress his friends, I leave the ring of my relatives above at the same time Cousin Sheldon and Rosalind are

leaving too, going to open air, perhaps dry land, and
descending to John's pit I have not only the measured
pleasure of seeing him, but also the flattery, which I don't
get at home, of being the center of new attention again.
Even my relatives must be amazed by my popularity. This
is a stranger who's calling me, part of the real world. I may
be as popular as the role I've played, the bad girl who's really good, the best of everyone else's worst, as if being popular is what really counts in life, surfaces, like my mother
tried to teach me as a little kid: *Don't be yourself, act nice!*
Popularity is what *they* think. But who am I to judge, as
Aunt Min said.

I may be better than I know.

Besides, the ooze and ease of myself, my body, astonishes me.

Nothing makes me uptight. In my no-bottoms but long
sparkle-sweater top, I reach out to John's heart enclosed
under a white pique shirt and tight vest and see his knees
lock together demurely, but I can't help kidding him. "You
look like a little wedding-cake man, John, that's the effect
you have for me. You look perched!"

He puts his hands over my eyes.

"You're not my cousin too, are you?" I shriek, because
that *would* be a coincidence. "Why are you here?"

"I'm a waiter," he says. "You look pretty weird yourself."

I try to hide my uncertainty, a growing fear, and laugh,
timing myself to the laughter of his friends in tuxedos too.

Upstairs: "Aunt Min, where did Cousin Kadey go?"

Suddenly, I feel as if I've stumbled into an all-male convention, aware that other people are on this boat, not just
my family. And from this distance my relatives sound
drunk, demanding.

"Aunt Min, who do you like better, Cousin Kadey or do
you like me?"

"I like you both the same."

Blood darkens behind my eyes, throbs sensually. John lets go. Nothing is different down here, except it's darker. I see flashes of red. I pose, confused. I lift my sweater over my head. Lit up by the swinging lamp behind, and raising my arms, my breasts in profile cause a shadow on the ship's wall, full, ripened and tipped with an extended nipple. In the dark woodiness of the long curved room, John's white-blond hair has turned peachy, his cheeks are red, his neck thickens. He turns floral too, far peachier than I remember him actually. But I can't be scared. I search his eyes, pressing my face to his, breathing his used air. His eyes shut. He strains to be unseen by me. He strokes my hips. But so thin is John's skin that fishy quivers dart behind his lids, giving him away.

"You don't like me!" I cry out, accusing, trying to trick him.

But I know it's true. He's using me for his friends.

"I'd rather tell jokes," he admits jokingly, in a John Wayne drawl, the the old black-and-white movie lawman teaching sense about where I don't belong. "But a man's got to do what a man's got to do."

"You're afraid!"

My mocking, little-girl familiarity, my intimacy with these strange men is my big mistake. I'm being made a fool. Though in reality, I don't mind.

"Care for a refill on drinks?" John asks pleasantly, changing his tone now, laughing lightly. He pours ale for himself, blowing the foam off. "Well, down the hatch!"

All the men drink up.

Cousin Morton, his dark, thick-featured face slack from hanging downwards, loose lips parted lasciviously, showing a gleam of tooth, eyes rolling, peers through the door above me, crouched on his hands and knees, trying to see what is happening. I ignore him maliciously, out of spite.

"She's so bad," my relatives are saying about me, admiringly. But for the rest of the world I might be too bad. Or too good. How can I tell?

Down here in the thicker air with the engine vibrating, you can't hear the singing, the distant band playing, only a few whines, muffled by the smell of farts and beer. What should I do now? Talk naturally, not act scared, at least try? Walk away? My relatives think I'm deserting them anyway. Can Newton ever believe I'm shy now? Everywhere, above, below, except for the sky which is dark too, water is rocking me.

But John grows easier, having proved his point. He raises his glass to me. "So Kadey, so Kadey," he repeats. "You're still sticking at the same job? A person only has one life. You ought to try everything, like me." Then he remembers he's a waiter again. "Have you had enough to eat? A dinner mint possibly? Coffee? A spot of tea?"

My own shadow excites me, the cartoon lady of my childhood dreams in front of so many men. Cupping breasts, older, heavier than I wish unless I keep my arms raised, I strut forward, lick John under his chin, slick and soften a bit of bypassed stubble and loosen his collar, although at first he resists. His skin tastes bitter along the jaw, but buttery, oleaginous where I find a slight pouch and I think of early summer time and daisies and particularly the innocent brightness and reflection of buttercups, pollen dust sprinkling.

"John, John, darling," I hear myself whispering.

And what does he hear?

"'Atta-boy, John, John-buddy!" his friends call.

Vibrations stop. The boat tilts gently. John tickles me
with fingers behind my knees until I bend, unsteady, then
closes my hand over his hard prick, unzipping, hiding the
pallid dwarf. He says, "Do you think you're too good for
me?" John instructs me quietly to begin pumping. "This
is for you, no, for me, yes, for you, no, for me . . ." he
breathes harshly.

Morton, hunching, narrates to relatives unseen, a low
buzz, only their feet on view, the family feet, naked, narrow, with overly-long second and third toes, a bunion here,
another foot fully shod.

Why, I wonder? Falling to my knees.

Every year I leave the Cousins' Club and think I'll never
come back again, I'm too dependent on it, knowing myself
through my kin. But I can't resist.

"Do as I say," commands John.

I clasp his buttock which is tensing beneath folds of
material, scratching my hands. That he remains dressed
excites me. It's not modest, it's obscene. I didn't plan this,
but what the hell, I shrug exultantly. Let everybody watch!
What can I lose? My self-control? As long as they're
watching me I'm safe, protected by their vigilance, no matter what I do or feel. I act for us all. The boat tosses lightly, as if shivering. We tip over. Everything is upside down.
No wonder I need them. Yes! Dependency sets me free,
and I shout, "Look! This is for me!"

WATCHBIRDS

Ever since Leo went away to his conference in Albany and I found the downstairs door open but nothing taken, I thought I was being watched. This is nothing new. I've been afraid of somebody I didn't know and wasn't pre-pared for spying on me for a long time, ever since I was a child, since the days when they were watching me, con-stantly comparing: "Ellen does . . . this," and "Ellen does . . . that," my mother explained me to her friends while I was supposed to be sleeping in my nursery-rhyme motif bedroom, where Jack jumped over the candlestick on the floor, and the old woman who lived in a shoe wrung her hands up and down the red curtains. But I was really eavesdropping. Many times I heard the story of how my father in the hospital broad-armed the poor doctor the day I was born, pushing his way into a room full of screaming infants with his camera and tape measure, bending over and checking reflexes, length and coloring—not just mine, but other babies, too—comparing me even then. ("How else would I know you were normal?" he defends himself now. "You were my first baby!") On the living room rug, I remember playing alone, turning a pencil around between my fingers, and a voice from nowhere, a purple face around the corner, yelling down at me: "Drop that pencil right now! Don't you dare stick that pencil up between your legs. Why can't you be nice like your little sister?" My first book, *Manners Can Be Fun*, featured a bird on every page and a moral: THIS IS THE WATCHBIRD, WATCHING YOU!

Besides, it's not just that I thought I was being watched by whoever broke into the downstairs apartment; I worried that I was being listened to. And even that didn't worry me right away. It took Olivia to convince me of it, to make me believe that there was something real I could be frightened over.

That and the fact that when Leo came home from Albany that night, he announced, glumly, "Somebody's been through my private papers. Did you do this?"

"No."

"Hmmm, they must have actually come in then. This box I keep my records in looks a little like a money box. Strange they didn't take anything." I'd already checked. We still owned our laptops, our stereo system, DVD, and our TV. Eighty dollars for grocery shopping still sat neatly folded under a saltshaker. "They could have taken our money, and didn't."

"How do you know anyone was here then?"

He pulled back the lid on his strongbox and showed me the disarray. Notes strewn, helter-skelter. But Leo's not neat, Leo could have made this mess himself, despite his pride that he's so organized. He turned suddenly. "Say, why are my binoculars on top of the desk? Were you using them?"

I shrieked. For the first time, my stomach leaped, my heart bellyflopped. Another clue.

When I first came down from my studio that morning and discovered the door askew, opened partway, I thought I was the one who'd unlocked it, that in the middle of the night when I was downstairs retrieving my book, half-stoned and enjoying myself, pigging out on a Veniero's chocolate-covered pastry—taking advantage of the fact that there was no Leo to look pretty for this week—that I'd been careless with his part of the house, that I must be the phantom burglar who was frightening myself, creeping in. Especially since it had happened before, too—a year ago, when I called the police and they kicked the unlocked door down, showing me later the scraping of a picked lock, long scratches. "It's not your imagination, Lady," they swore to me. But what would you say if you'd just kicked somebody's door down? And now, going down for the mail in my flannel nightgown, finding the door swaying, recalling that last night I'd been down there, I was convinced of my guilt. I'd come back and thrown the mail on the table for Leo, and looked around, reassuring myself, checking under the clawfoot bathtub, behind armchairs, half-turning in the dim light before I saw that a piece of wood was sticking out of the lock. And I knew this immediately: if I had done that, jammed the lock with evidence that way, I wouldn't have forgotten about it.

I thought: What if somebody is still inside?

There was no way to reach Leo. Couldn't somebody be waiting for me?

In the hallway, I collared our neighbor, Michael, whispering, "Leo's door is open. I'm afraid that somebody's still in there, hiding."

My neighbor squinted at me, angry-eyed. An artist who thinks nobody appreciates him enough, he over-reacts. He can't stand being rejected, so he's always the one who does it. "What do you want me to do?"

Obviously, he wasn't going to search the place for me.

"Wait here and hold the keys." I'd gone in myself.

"Maybe whoever it was came in and got scared off," Leo answered me that night, answering only because I kept repeating my questions, close up and into his ear; he hates ambiguities. He doesn't like to be pushed. He doesn't like speculating about matters he can't pin down. "I think whoever it was left before they could take anything. They heard you on the stairs and got scared and ran out."

"Where'd they go? I would have seen them. How'd they get out?" The windows lock from inside.

He turned and rubbed his hair back, smacking his palm against his tall forehead. "How should I know? Am I a thief? At least I didn't lose anything. That's good."

"But how come you're sure that they were in here then?"

"Because everything's different, that's how. It's obvious."

The intrusion doesn't seem to bother him. It bothers me a lot, somebody jamming the lock so that if Leo or I tried to get in while they were inside they wouldn't be trapped there. But when I press Leo, really press him, he explains his theory that when "the thieves" came in there might have been a mutual recognition of renegades, that they took one peek at his stack of social policy books, the ones about utopian communities that he's written himself, his notes, his calendar and his clothes, and felt an alliance with him—his calendar shows he's at a world-poverty conference ("*Bro! My man!*" he imagines them exclaiming exultantly)—an explanation so blatantly romantic and race-ridden and ridiculous, with so many crazy mistakes about who's robbing whom and why, that even he ends up laughing at it, making fun of himself, a trait I love about

him. He says that he's got to joke about it because I won't.
"Don't take yourself so seriously," he warns.

"You don't think I did it?" I ask him.

He hugs me. "Of course not."

"Without remembering it?" I confess. "I was stoned."

"Who cares?" He shakes his long head, hair glinting
with show-offy brass highlights when he finally sits down,
his voice warm but suddenly thick with exhaustion from
his long train ride, his tiring week of politicking for grant
money, too exhausted to pay attention to me.

My head bobs. I lean into him. I've missed him a lot.
"Because I would have remembered the part about sticking
the wood in."

Obviously, his explanation about the crooks coming and
thinking he had good politics, good taste, was an anti-
answer. Like reverse magnets, so to speak; reason's opposite. Was he worrying?

"Maybe somebody's coming to check on you, Leo," I
venture the next morning, changing the pillowcases.

"Why me? Why not on you?" he asks over breakfast.

"It's your part of the house." We divide things equally,
spaces and property, a studio for me and a separate apartment downstairs for Leo, a duplex of sorts in this crazy
New York real estate market, we reasoned when we first
came across it, a great rental, even though we have to share
the hallway with other tenants. But anybody who knows
enough to spy on Leo knows that. The studio is mine and
downstairs is Leo's. "But if they're spying on us, whoever's doing it is in worse shape than they think they are. We
don't know anything." I'm speaking loudly. I'm talking

directly into the floral arrangement. "What can they be listening for?"

"You're nuts."

The next day, I read in the newspaper about a screw-on
receiver cap that lights up red if your phone's tapped. I
refuse to buy it for $79.98. But if I'm nuts, I tell Leo,
there's an even nutsier paranoid market out there.

Christo and Julie, old friends, and Olivia, another dear
friend, are over at the house one night just before
Christmas. Snow is falling outside, and we're wrapping
presents, excited by a sense of wonderful potentialities, a
new season for us, until Olivia and Christo begin a heavy
discussion about art, which Olivia considers her domain,
and Olivia accuses Christo of presenting gender constructs
that are male dominant, although the usual struggle for
personal dominance is all covert with her. She disguises
her maneuvers as aesthetic politics. Olivia is an art critic.
She is full of theories. She explains to Christo in measured
half-tones about perception, how reality exists outside the
object and event, about how the object "merely signifies,
merely carries," the meaning, the perceptual cues. "Clues,
I suppose you'd call them," she says, trying to create
drama. "And our observation of them as interpreters.
We're all the artists ultimately. The viewer constructs. It's
the way we put the pieces together. Contextualize. We're
the one's who create."

Christo considers this typically female have-it-both-ways
thinking, although he leaves out the word "female" when
he suggests it. A poet, after all, doesn't he know about
artists? Julie's a painter. Doesn't he live with her? "What

do you mean, that meaning doesn't exist? That's an academic construct. Art carries its own meaning."

"You don't understand me," Olivia shouts. She bends forward in the leather director's chair. "You don't know what I'm saying and you don't even know you don't know it." She sighs and clicks her tongue once. "God."

Leo sighs too—even academic political people get bored easily by this kind of thing, "aesthetic athletics," Leo calls it—and Julie's worried, afraid that if Christo gets too worked up, he's going to pick a fight with her later, after they leave.

Olivia says to Christo, "The issue's psychological. Humans are always interpreting, actually, because they just can't help it. We're look-ers, seers and be-ers, subject and object, both at the same time, and the artist creates works that implore our subject's participation. It's an ongoing shift between artists and viewer through the medium of context, the matrix of event."

"Hey, want to hear a funny story?" I interrupt her. I hope the story's funny only because Leo always laughs at me about it. She can't say no; I'm the hostess. But I hope she's not mad. Julie's happy, and Leo's happy too, but he won't show it if it doesn't work. I launch into the story about the phantom robbery four months ago, the robbery that never was, while I'm serving roasted peppers and salad. ("More wine?" Leo's asking gaily, holding up a bottle. It's working. But Olivia thinks I'm a clod.) Afterwards, I stretch back on the couch under the Victorian lamp, totally exhausted.

"You never found anybody?"

"They never took anything?"

"Not that we can discover," Leo tells our guests.

"I even thought that I was the one who did it," I suggest, still willing to play the buffoon. "I have the type of personality that makes me feel guilty about everything."

"That's silly," Olivia says. "If you're guilty of everything, you must think you're God."

"That is the way she is," Julie explains me to Christo, who nudges her. Julie and I used to be in a women's leadership group together. She thinks my ambivalences are funny, the way I end up balancing everything out to zero, strategic debits and credits, that I'm a laugh riot, practically. "Ellen wants to think she's in control of something."

Olivia: "Who doesn't?"

Christo (sarcastically): "Does this relate to art theory?"

"Who do you think could have robbed me?" I interject speedily.

"They didn't rob you. They robbed Leo," Olivia corrects me, a stickler for constants.

"They didn't rob me, because they didn't take anything," Leo re-corrects.

"Yes, but the fact that they were inside the house. Isn't that a psychological robbery?"

Leo shrugs. No grudges, as usual.

"Yes, yes," I'm nodding. I try to share Leo's joke. "Leo says they didn't take anything because they looked at the private stuff he had and felt a connection to his interests and value system. Anyway," I say, reverting to the familiar, "If they're watching us, well, whoever is doing it is in worse shape than they think they are."

"Things might be worse than you think," Olivia answers. "Who says they're not? Maybe they're compiling information."

"In Greece, years ago when I was a child, everybody was under surveillance until after the junta . . . " Christo begins.

"You might be saying that about things being worse off just to protect yourself," Julie guesses. "I'll bet you think they really are watching you."

"Leo's account is nonsensical," Olivia says with finality. "If anything, it's your very values that keep you under surveillance. Whoever *them* is, your values are certainly not what keeps *them* away from you."

"But who could have done it?" Talking about our discovery, I become re-involved in the puzzle. "It couldn't be crooks, because they didn't take anything. It couldn't be an accident because there was actually wood jammed into the lock, splinters of evidence. And it couldn't be the Government—I mean the Military and the FBI, and the CIA, they aren't supposed to do that kind of thing anymore—they have no reason to do that kind of thing here anyway, and especially since it was all done too crudely." I laugh, uneasy, because I'm building a plot that has too many holes in it. "I'm sure that any secret agency would have more class, more finesse, they probably have special keys for picking these locks, they don't need to stick pieces of wood in it."

"Why not? Sounds like one of the secret agencies to me," Olivia says, probably getting even with me for interrupting her, not allowing her to save face in front of Christo. "What makes you think they wouldn't be crude?"

"No." Leo speaks abruptly. "This isn't TV."

"I remember the time we had anti-world trade activists living in this building and the FBI came to check. Very suave. Central casting for the FBI. Summer suits and maroon ties," I say to her. "They didn't seem sloppy."

But the argument is finished for her. Pieces of arugula hang from her mouth before her tongue slips carefully, quickly, beneath, and she swallows. "So. It must be the

FBI. So," she repeats. "The authorities were here already. Well, what are you guilty of?"

"Nothing!" I'm surprised to find Leo and me shouting in unison. I didn't know he cared.

"Nothing?" The whole story, Olivia's new power to make us flinch, strikes her as funny this time, and she continues the interrogation playfully. "Isn't everybody guilty of something. Innocence, for sure, is hard to believe."

Christo looks glum. If it's really a federal authority, his distinctive Greek accent is much too recognizable. He doesn't yet have a green card.

"What did they do then?" I ask Olivia, feeling helpless.

"How do I know? Probably, they planted a bug. That's standard, so think about it. Every word you say is on record. Everything counts. There's no way of getting away from it, Ellen."

"Shhhhhhh."

"They know your name already," she smirks at me. And I don't want to agree with her, to tell that I've been thinking about that for a long, long time.

"Where did they plant it?" I'm whispering.

Then I notice that everybody is staring at the Victorian lamp, its swoops of gold, its swags and flounces. The lamp looks innocent. But then so does everybody. Suddenly I'm furious with Olivia.

"How can you sit here in my house and be so glib about intrusion?" I yell at her. "How dare you, how dare you!"

"If you're not guilty there's nothing they can do to you." Olivia is still playing.

"How can you be so glib about the fact that people who are just minding their own business are under surveillance—which, by the way, I don't believe?"

"I'm teasing." She sighs. "Don't be so touchy. Don't be so overwrought. In real ways we're all under surveillance, both internal and external, aren't we? It happens to the best of us."

She's trying to disguise her voice though, I notice. Low and gruff with a Spanish R-trill, pretending to be a man. We're all suddenly talking in funny voices, it occurs to me. All three of my guests, and Leo too, get up abruptly, leave the room, and Leo helps them with their coats. At the doorway, everybody contrives to sound innocent, as normal as possible, laughing and flattering each other and wishing each other Good Christmases, kissing one another upon the cheeks—" "When can we get together again?" "Soon, soon." "Yes, soon."—saying goodbye.

"Do you think there's any truth to it?" I whisper to Leo when we're alone, while he's taking off his clothes, straggling them around the room without thinking about it, dropping his socks, then lounging back on the couch, plumping the pillow up.

"Of course not. How many times are you going to ask me?"

"Never again," I whisper.

He laughs. He considers me a compulsive repeater. "Promise?"

I nod.

"Then come here, Ellen, Ellen Burke Eliason Goldsmith," he says to me.

"Call me Madison," I tell him. "I'm changing my name. I read that Madison is a very popular name this season."

"Come here, Madwoman, I mean Madison."

We both laugh. He pulls the cord on the lamp, making the room dark. I like the darkness, the snow still falling outside, on the other side of the windowpane, but I doubt if this act of unplugging the lamp, if this disconnects our secret listener.

"Do you think that if somebody were listening they'd find me interesting?" I ask him.

"I doubt it."

That's just what I'm afraid of. What is there to talk about, what is there to say that will make a difference to anybody. Nothing worth guarding, which is the loneliness of it. We roll over on the couch, face to face, tooth on back and claws on buttocks, animals conscious of their own sounds, creating meaning from them, pasted to each other with the secrets of our own pelts, no words necessary and yet, and yet, the pleasure of them: "I love you." "I love you, too." But nothing new here. If they were listening, they've now disconnected themselves, I'm positive of it. But just in case, for the record in case there is a record, just as Leo pushes himself into me hard, it occurs to me to yell. I yell loud, high-pitched, rippling with sounds that are intended to crack their ear-drums, to pierce the tympanum, unbalancing the middle ear, to keep them from ever paying attention to me again, and besides, I am not boring, I'm perfectly self-sufficient, I'm unique, I am so worth watching. *Listen to me because* . . . *oh, yes . . . .oh, yes, yes . . . yes,*" I'm shouting . . . .

Which is not my usual practice. But this time it's like boasting, a sound so loud that it turns out onto itself, tremors that shift, shapes that create new meanings, a sound so loud I'll never have to listen to myself again.

"Wooo," Leo says afterwards, holding me, his breath a warm nest surrounding me. "That was wonderful."

"It was?"

"Wasn't it?"

Like a television, switched off, we cool down and glow mildly at each other.

"Thank you."

We squeeze each other in the darkness. "No, darling. Thank you."

Just in case they're listening. Yes. This is how we should do it.

"Can it hurt anybody, being polite?" my mother used to say. My father agreed with her, naturally. But why were they always fighting. "We never fight, don't say that to people." She would look down at the floor, the soiled underwear, and ask, "What if a car would smash into your house right now, into your living room and you both had to go to the hospital. Aren't you ashamed?"

"Can I get you a glass of water, Sweetheart?

"Yes, please."

"My pleasure."

"Thank you very much."

LOVE YOURSELF

The bellboy at the door, named Juan, five feet tall, intimidates me. The desk man, grinning, flashing white tombstone teeth in a long face, scares me too. Juan brings me coffee. I stay in my room. Outside, through the tall glass, palm trees fling graceful fronds, a processional. Sunlight dazzles. Waves play. And people. Inside, I overflow my bed. I walk earnestly. Which is to say, without grace. Tides pull the dancing sea forward, then back again, imperceptibly. Trepidation pulls me in, sucks me down, all that I am and see, and won't let me out again.

Tomorrow I will be a new woman.

Tomorrow I will undergo beauty surgery.

That's right, I won a scholarship to a fat farm from my Love Yourself group. You shouldn't make fun of it. Nobody lost weight for me, you know. Dr. Pater only made the final arrangements. I was the one who lost weight, who fasted, who suffered to condense—until I became loveable.

I'm not loveable yet, actually. But I love myself. That's the difference. The sigh, the heave, the sulk and bulk of me. And now, months later, flesh drapes from my proud bones reflecting and absorbing tropical light like the finest damask in the Governor's palace, soft as deep velvet, in sensual folds, crushed plush to the touch yet iridescing where the sun glows, my stretchmarks gleaming like opalescent skeins, so that I can't resists stroking myself and wondering why: Why do they want to cut all this away? Standards of beauty? I hate to give anything up.

That's part of the problem, naturally. Dr. Pater warned me to be prepared when I changed my looks. "If you lose weight, you must deal with emptiness, the fact of your limitations."

"I don't want to."

"Of course not." He laughed indulgently. "You want to hang on to your omnipotence. Illusions of it. You're being deliberately childish."

"Childlike," I correct him.

"What's the difference? You know what I mean." He really meant infantile. From his big leather chair in the center of the room, perfectly shaped and padded to his slouched posture, he tosses an impatient arm, hairy and tanned, and pinpoints me for the group. "Classical resistance!" he glares. And cues them.

"Such a pretty face—"

"Look how she sits. The power spot in the corner of the couch, trying to pretend that she loves herself."

"What's all that fat hiding?"

"She's afraid that if she loses weight she'll have to deal with her sexuality."

"What're you talking about? I've slept with almost everyone in this group. At least I don't have to worry about what the refrigerator is thinking about me!"

"You didn't sleep with me," a woman named Debby whines, injustice collecting. She knows I mean the men.

Dr. Pater says nothing. He disapproves. "Love yourself. Let this message fill you every day, day by day."

The desk man nodded, contemptuously calling out to Juan, beast of burden and humpbacked under my half-dozen suitcases when I moved in. From the artificial light and shadows of his chromium and glass booth, where he registers the old, the rich, the impotent, the sagging and the insecure, he is dreaming now of the beach outside. Nubile girls in string bikinis romp. Will I ever be one of them? After tomorrow, possibly. But only if the scars fade.

In a sterile room, in an intimate reconstruction of who I am, the beauty surgeon slices and splices and folds back the flesh, puts his hands in and takes out dozens and dozens of little people, perfectly proportioned and expressive, petrified, ossified, but not fetuses, adults. Tiny adults, fully dressed, who have been living or dead inside of me, which surprises me very much. I don't know about it until I come to under the cool lights, and I see them floating in corked bottles, in tubes, like darling freaks from fly-by-night freak shows and county fairs I loved when I was a kid, except there's nothing freakish here. These pickled people are perfectly ordinary, familiar, dun-colored and thin-lipped like my Midwestern grade school teachers; high-boned and handsome, like my first love; they look like my mother, my father, aunts, uncles, friends and grandparents, my fresh fruit and vegetable man; an unpleasant account executive I once worked for with poisonous pimples on his brow. The only freakish part is the fact that they are smaller than usual; wee folks, like fingerlings.

"Where did they come from?" I ask the beauty surgeon, imagining all of them in there flailing and disagreeing with each other, vying over lobes of liver and slopes of stomach

to be taken care of. No wonder I weighed so much! Or
that I had to eat to meet their needs!

Don't know, the beauty surgeon murmurs behind his
mask. Perhaps he's marveling. *Strange case.*

He skirts my skin with a scissors, skewering me and
immobilizing me like a stripped turkey. This nimble last
stitchery is choreographed under local anesthesia with my
cooperation. He stresses the necessity of future starvation,
the strictest dieting.

I'm worried about losing my self-control. What if I can't
help myself? It frightens me. I need a wide margin for failure.

"Leave big seams!" I'm shouting.

Bending, glinting, the beauty surgeon goes *snip* . . . .

The wounds heal. I wave goodbye to Juan, goodbye to the
shiny desk man, leaving a big tip. Against the brilliant vast
sky, in the vasty breeze, silhouetted, I hail a cab for the air-
port. My old clothes remain behind.

Back in my Love Yourself group, everyone is thrilled that
I'm so cute, my lavender-edged body, scars like rick-rack
trim, so shapely and so delicate.

"You look great!"

"Fantastic!"

"Utterly gorgeous and self-fulfilled!"

They all shout, chorusing each other.

"Thank you, thank you," I acknowledge, self-admiring. Slightly
embarrassed, but terribly pleased. To think that I used to believe
that I could actually learn to love myself the way I was born.

"Are you sure that being this beautiful isn't too threatening for you?" Dr. Pater asks me, neutrally. "That's what
we're here for. To work things out. To make sure you don't
feel threatened. We're going to work on separating true

self-love from narcissism next. And grandiosity. Nothing should be too grand for you. Are you unhappy being smaller? Do you ache with a new kind of emptiness?"

Despite Dr. Pater's flat questions—flat because he doesn't want to show public favoritism—he's proud of me. He plans to present a paper about me at the next professional conference: Symptoms, Symbiosis and the Struggling Image of Self: A Sure Cure. He wants to protect me though. He doesn't want the others to be jealous of me. I understand this. We exchange deep looks. I don't even have to say a word.

But amazingly, after awhile I gain weight again, and Dr. Pater's conference paper is threatened. Self-sabotage, or hostility? Dr. Pater accuses me of both.

I go home, weeping.

I arrive earlier than the others on the next night, and Dr. Pater greets me, a nod of disappointment and undisguised scorn. "What are you eating? Let's get some reality on all this." He shambles across his thick carpeting and sees my teeth working up and down, suspects I'm salivating, and grows firm. He places a heavy hand on my shoulder where there's no long cushioning, where no excess flesh folds up and I am taut, where nerve ends fork and galvanize at his touch; excruciating. "You have something in your mouth, don't you?"

My jaws work convulsively, reacting. "Only teeth."

I feel like I did in third grade when the teacher asked me if I was chewing gum.

"Open up, please. I'd like to believe you."

"This is degrading. You can't order me around."

"Relax and trust me. Incorporate my wisdom. That's what I'm here for. Now open!"

"You can't make me. I have boundaries."

"Come on!"

He strokes my hair paternally, tilting my head backwards, gentle but definite and for my own good, and puts a thick thumb between my mandibles, knuckling up under my nose, pulls at my jaw, then quickly slips his hand into a fist to pull my hair back. My lips, my mouth, I am wide open for him. What does he see? I imagine a flushed pink, shadowed cavern of throat, lovely and delicate, glistening curves and hollows, the gentle beckoning darkness of an inner world. He sticks his head up close. Closer, looming over me, and lowers his eye. He peers inside. His eyelash tickles my lip. He leans closer. My mouth shuts, then clamps. He slides in easily, although with hard thrusts, head-first and salty with sweat, kicking, crying out. Then both he, from within, and I, emit low moans of rumbling pleasure. His, muffled, of course, resonant, but soon absorbed. My own, longer, soon grow tremulous.

Afterwards, I lie back on his chair, alone, undulating.

The group comes in one by one, some people late. Naturally, a few resisting. They fight for seats, display the way they've grown to love themselves by elbowing each other out of the way. Week after week, a real family.

"Say, where's Dr. Pater? Usually he's early. You know, I can't get over how satisfied you look. You look like a new woman."

"You certainly do," Debby says. "You look great."

"Thank you." My voice is perfectly modulated, the low growl of love, so different from hunger. I smile, show teeth. My mother always told me that my smile was my best feature. My teeth are straight and strong.

SOME CHRISTMASES

I'm sick, it's three days before Christmas, and raining into yesterday's snow. Ben's at work and when I look into the mirror while brushing my teeth I remember suddenly that I dreamed last night of turning into a fifty-four year-old woman with coarse moustaches and a rogue hair curling blackly on my neat chin. But I'm only thirty-five.

I go back to sleep, nestling with the cat, who struggles slightly, then begins to purr.

This time I dream it's night and summer and I'm following friends single-file on stilts on a narrow wooden walkway down to the ocean. It's foggy. "Go without me, I'll catch up," I shout, waiting behind for a young man with round tortoise-shell glasses who nobody else in our group likes, a social misfit, bobbing his head on a skinny neck and smiling. Actually, I don't want to be seen with him either. But I can't help liking him myself. I respect his intelligence. Alone on the beach, kneeling at the foot of a sand rise, he demonstrates a long, rubbery black tube-like machine he's developed for getting him out of dangerous situations. That's the reason he's late. He forgot it. He presses a button and the tube rises and jumps forward like a big worm.

It lands on top of the dune. "In case of attack or emergency I can ride this," he explains proudly. The wind blows his oily hair straight back. I nod. But what good is it really, I wonder. Is it practical? It only jumps short distances and up low heights. Any truly dangerous animal or person or a bullet could jump that far too. "Now if you could just travel inside the tube, enlarge it a little so we could hide, that's another story," I suggest cautiously.

For the past two weeks a homeless woman has been living under the inside front steps in our small apartment building, a white-haired woman with heavy-lidded black eyes and extraordinary sculpted cheekbones. This is not a dream. She reclines on a five-gallon can of paint behind the radiator at night, reading books that I can't see the titles of without appearing rude, pulling at her tweed coat. She moved in while I was flat on my back, Ben tells me, by entering the lobby and pressing in so close behind tenants at the door that it was impossible to keep her out except by force. Now, apparently, someone has given her a downstairs key. Not me. When she first arrived, she carried a quilt, but the handyman threw it out. So she shoulders a plastic shopping bag, and sleeps with her head in her lap.

"I don't want to go to Joanne and Paul's party tonight," Ben complains, throwing his coat on a chair and dumping his briefcase on top of it. "I'm tired and my throat's sore. I think I'm catching your flu. At least you've been in bed all day."

"We have to go, whether you want to or not, and even if we're both sick. It's not a party really, it's a showing of Paul's painting at Paul's loft—which is not a loft really," I explain because Ben doesn't know them that well, "—but a five-room tenement apartment on the fringes of

Chinatown because Paul can't afford a loft since all of the lofts have been taken over by lawyers and businessfolk, and successful dot-com-types."

At the party, Maxine, Paul's agent, gestures with a slice of focaccia and pushes by me in the doorway. "You've lost a lot of weight." She sucks in her cheeks for illustration.

"I can't eat, I'm nauseous. I have a virus, I'm sick."

"You're emptying the room," Ben comments, which is true. People are fading away from me like a chorus after a big number in a Broadway show. But at least I can see the paintings now, where before I couldn't; bright surfaces of dots and grids.

Molly Karp, who I haven't seen in two years, since her divorce, pulls me into the tiny kitchen and tells me about a terrible affair she'd been having with a woman dentist. "It's so good to be back in New York. Here, at least, I can get some distance on it."

"Why are you having an affair with a dentist?" I ask, really meaning the word "woman." But I don't want to be too personal.

"Actually, she's an artist, a wonderful photographer. Dentist is my word for someone my mother would have wanted me to marry."

"I just heard that Nathaniel has been on the fire escape smoking a joint!" Joanne, in a satin tuxedo jacket, strides angrily into the room where her twelve-year old son sits, legs dangling, on top of the refrigerator, cradling a portable TV.

"Mom, it was a regular cigarette. Don't you think I can tell the difference?" Nathaniel shouts down.

"He's shy with adults, that's all," I soothe. "He's staying out of everyone's way."

"I was mugged at gunpoint yesterday," our old friend A.J. tells Ben, conversationally. "My shop director's daughter was stabbed last week."

"Seems like folks are getting more and more desperate out in the world. The economy, unbelievably high apartment prices, everyone's holding on to what they have."

I tell A.J. and Joanne and Molly about the woman who lives under our stairs. "The thing that kills me is that this woman could be any one of us down on our luck, out of money. She's been forced into the streets because landlords who were warehousing apartments evicted her on some technicality when they converted into condos. And she's a regular person. I mean she's not a crazy lady, she's clean and lucid and nice."

"How do you know she's nice?" Ben looks at me curiously.

"Maybe she's my friend Maggie's friend who used to write for The New Yorker and then turned into a shopping-bag lady!" Joanne cries. "I'd call Maggie but she's in Majorca for three weeks."

Ben and I take a taxi home and drink Calvados. We both have fevers. In bed, clutching separate pillows, I dream that we're floating on a blue lake. Ben's body, rippling and long, silver-striped, is lying partially on top of my body. He takes off my bathing suit, bottoms only because people lounging on the grassy beach might see, and the sky surrounds us, brilliant, depthless and rich. The sand is gold at the water's edge. We float backwards, backwards, with tiny neons darting past our knees. My cheek rests against his arm. I notice a dark patch beneath me; moss. Is it undulating? But humping forward in an eel's entwined curve, we avoid it gracefully, scraping gently on sand and stones.

When the alarm rings, Ben rises. I dream I'm awake, that he's kissing me, tracking me like a sea flower with his open mouth. I jump upright and shout: "Wait! I can't take advantage of you. You have to go to work."

The woman who lives under the stairs goes out on week-days and Saturdays, but now that it's holiday season she stays all day. Of course she probably has no place, not even a sen-ior center or community shelter to go to, or a back room where a storekeeper lets her sit on a box, like Mary Hecker's brother-in-law made me sit waiting for her once while I was in college because I looked too punky. But the stores are too busy for her. In and out, in and out. "You're taking up space, we need to get those boxes, we can't keep moving you around," the stockboys complain. "You're sitting on good merchandise." The owner kicks her out. Ben and I come home from shopping at Lord & Taylor's laden with boxes, gifts, both useful and useless, wrapping paper poking out of our bags. In front of the radiator, a parked bike blocks the old woman from view, fortunately. Can she see me?

But upstairs, guilt or empathy takes hold. I go back down again and peek over and ask, "Would you like some food?"

"Yes, thank you very much." Dignified, she looks up, over handle-bars and the high grill. Her white hair is pulled back. She lifts deepset eyes. She could have been a dancer, possibly. But then I've never seen her move.

On the other side of the glass door, in the marble lobby, two street kids in headbands sit on our low threshold fix-ing a radio by pulling its back off. Always, lately, and for the first time in many years, we're seeing homeless people again. Soon the radio blares hip-hop loudly up the stairs, right through my door where, in my own kitchen, I'm preparing a chicken sandwich and find only the smallest amount of mayonnaise in the refrigerator. "Make sure there's enough left for me," Ben says from behind his Journal of American History. I slice an orange, add cookies to the paper plate, and make tea. "Don't let those punks see you feeding her," he jokes. "Or you'll have every street kid in the neighborhood lining up to be fed."

"Doesn't it bother you?"

He glares back. If the personal is political, there's a political contradiction somewhere. "Of course it does, what do you think. But our home's the only place we have that's ours." He opens the door, since I'm balancing plates. "Face it, you can't take everybody in."

Ben has to work late on Christmas Eve, of all things, and I'm still sick but mobile, anyway, feeling disconnected inside myself. We're spending Christmas with Ben's father and sister and brother-in-law in Connecticut tonight, and I've just finished wrapping gifts when the doorbell rings. I ignore it. Who would I want to see? It rings again. Short, short, *long*, repeated. As if signalling. Instead of pressing the buzzer, I get the idea of tiptoeing down in my nightgown, ducking my head below the landing to look. There, in a Burberry duffle stands Rennie Williams who I haven't seen in years, an old boyfriend of a friend who moved away. He's tall, freckled and gangly.

Instinctively, I back up fast. What is he doing here?

But he sees me anyway. He grins and waves. I frown, then squint, dissembling, to show I have no idea . . . who is this man? He laughs with disbelief, brows flaring, shakes his head comically, flinging his arm in a *y'all come*—so it seems too rude to resist then. Obviously he knows that I see him. Knowledge leads to consequences. He calls my name.

What is it Barbara told me about him? He's a good lover?

"Rennie!" I cry, as if surprised, opening the door a scant foot and blocking it. "Rennie? I didn't recognize you. It's been ten years."

"I could tell you didn't know me."

Up close, on the outside at least, he's unchanged, innocent and a little goofy and goodlooking, gentle but slightly seedy too; one of his lower molars is missing, and he seems genuinely hurt and disappointed when I tell him that he can't come in, that I'm busy because it's Christmas Eve. I don't mention Ben, because it's too complicated. He wouldn't remember him.

"Hey, I've been living in Cincinnati and I was here in New York and in your neighborhood and I thought I'd see how you were. I'll be here all week."

"I can always tell when it's Christmas because prodigals return to New York," I smile. "I'm sorry that I can't stand here talking, but there's a draft and I've got the flu. Look, my phone number's in the book." I'm lying, though. The phone is under Ben's name. In Cincinnati people are probably friendlier.

"Gee, you've been sick for a long time," the woman behind the radiator says, peering out, sympathetic.

Well, who knows if Rennie even lives in Cincinnati? I don't. He probably has a wife stashed back at the hotel too.

New sweaters and CD's and books and jewelry, gold Godiva boxes, I feel rich. Christmas is like a dream. My father-in-law gave me a burgundy satin nightgown from France with a lacy midriff, a gown that it turns out he also gave his girlfriend. I discovered this from a gleeful story he told about scandalizing the women behind him in line at Saks: "Look, Jessica! That man is buying two of the same sexy nightgowns in *different* sizes!" To Ben, in an aside during the turkey carving: "That's a nightgown a man has to live up to." I like the Oedipal undertones. Yet knowing my practical father-in-law, who hates shopping, I imagine that having found one good gift he thought matter-of-factly, "Well, why not two?" Anyway, I can't eat the chocolates and most of the clothes don't fit. When the old woman downstairs inquires about my Christmas, I don't reciprocate inquiries. "Fruitcake?" I offer her.

Back in our apartment, I sleep badly, panicked, lost in a dream on sleazy streets among glittering lights in a border-town in Mexico while Ben is parking the car. My shoes are missing and nobody else speaks Spanish. I wake, thinking about the woman downstairs.

So fastidious, I think. Where does she go to the bathroom? Last night, late, I heard a terrible commotion in the hall. A crook had gotten in and was stealthily gouging the lock. The woman sneaked out from behind the radiator and called the police. They wouldn't come because she wouldn't give her name and address. What address? So she got the boy upstairs to call. They caught the crook on the roof. In her smokey, New York-Irish, Hell's Kitchen accent, she speaks then admiringly of the police as she describes events: "Yes, and if they catch him here again they said they'll break his arm in three places."

Our friend Lex came over and left poetry, a Christmas present, under our door. "Your friend Lefty was here," the woman delivered the message to us. "I told her you were sleeping. I told her your husband was out."

"Evidently we have a doorman," Ben laughs. "Like our building is swanky."

But to me she's the perfect neighbor, that's how I see her, like the old days, supposedly, when everybody cared, or living in a small town. I can't go back to sleep. I imagine giving her our key so that she can use the toilet at least. Or in emergencies, she can use our phone. Yet once she's in, I know—even in my imagination—that we would grow friendlier and friendlier. Anna, her name is, I decide, rolling over fitfully. I never asked before because I was afraid of getting too involved. Overidentified, out of control. Anna, a nice name. Yes. After a Swedish nanny, like Ibsen's Nora in reverse? Ibsen's Nora was named after an Irish Nanny.

Anna is warm and sensible, that's what I like about her. Like Ben, but he can be so cold. When Anna smiles, it's like winter sunshine when no wind blows, suddenly surprising. "I once had a cat who looked just like this," she murmurs, picking up my kitten, praising his coat: striped and tortoise-swirled. Her lids lower gracefully. Her hands stroke fur. So I tell her the story of how I took my little cat to the medical center for his shot and how he cried pitifully non-stop on the bus where people smiled and caught my eye, even though some of the bus riders must have hated cats too and felt trapped. "The cat was in his cage?" I nod. She means "carrier." She chuckles at my chagrin when the clinic doctor tells me mine was the second cat treated there that morning with the same name.

"Boy, it's hard to name one of God's unique creatures," Anna sympathizes. "I remember I felt that naming Raskolnikov too, as if I had no right. And he didn't act like a Raskolnikov either, no brooding intellectual. He was a fat red cat, he let me carry him in my purse. We gave him food off the table and some we especially cooked. I called him Rascal, for short."

The word "we" and the story are so I'll understand the quality of her past home. I stop short of inquiring the circumstances, though; it would be rude. But she's lonely. Far lonelier than I'll ever be, I hope, no matter how sick, or if the city falls apart, and then she boasts how her cat lived to be twenty—"Quite old for a cat, we took wonderful care"—and I reciprocate by telling her about my last cat who died of a heart attack at 14 on the anniversary of Ben's mother's death while Ben and I were trying to give the cat its heart pill. "The vetinarian forced me to give him the pills, the cat hated pills, and angiograms too, instead of letting him die in peace. They knew he was dying to begin with. It cost a mint. He died in my arms. I heard the death rattle."

Anna's lips tighten. She's sad. "I know what you mean."

"Did *you* ever live on cat food?" I want to ask. Disgusting of me. How crass! Maybe I'd better ask her to stay. Instead: "I could have saved the life of half a starving Sudanese family for what the vet cost. It's a real racket."

"You know sometimes there's no heat in that radiator downstairs. I'm glad you invited me in."

"Oh, I hate being without heat. When Con Ed was working on the gas main outside, we didn't have heat. It makes you feel lonely."

Abruptly, Anna goes into the kitchen and makes us hot tea.

Ben's at work, luckily. I'm amazed to find out I'm so angry at him, I have no reason actually, he's always so sweet. It's not his fault, probably. We're overprotecting ourselves, as if it's too dangerous to love among strangers. Is it the times?

Anna and I sit opposite each other in the big gold wing chairs near the window under the hanging plants, and I think it would be nice if we had lace antimacassars, and little doilies on the end tables for our food. As if we were in the past already. I wonder if Anna can tat. There's a Victorian lamp. A pool of gold light lends the right touch.

"I was surprised you were so rude to your friend," Anna admits, stirring the cream, curving her pinky correctly. "But you had your reasons, you must have if you hadn't seen him in a long time. I know you."

"I can't explain." Does she really know me? "It's a feeling I have about letting him in, not anything he did, nothing I know for a fact."

"Perhaps your husband would have resented it. Yet your husband's a gentleman too."

Pleased, but puzzled by what I hear as a sudden trace of an English accent, and embarrassed too, though Anna doesn't disapprove, I look away, out the window. And there in the fresh snow, tromping in big boots, who do I see below, what a coincidence, but Rennie Williams again! Yes, Rennie Williams all right, and his collie dog and his good friend, carrying big shopping bags under the bank's black clock, and I know, intuitively, watching the dog's breath, that they're coming here. What would Ben say? Anna inside is bad enough. I panic. I mustn't let him in. What is that I heard about Rennie Williams from Barbara again? Yes, he's kind and generous. And he has a big curved prick. Naturally, I'm too courteous to mention any of this to

Anna, but I do shout, "Quick, Anna! Quick, turn out the lights, pretend I'm not home. We have to pretend, it's important. Please, please."

She looks uneasy. Doesn't move. Suspicious. "Why?"

A bad caretaker. "Because."

Kitchen lights, living-room lights, a bedroom light, one over the studio desk because it's winter, it's always so gloomy during the day, too many lights to turn off, and the bell rings. Anna buzzes back without using the intercom. Rennie's upstairs already, knocking at the door.

"Because my husband wouldn't like it," I whisper reluctantly; conveniently, knowing her respect for institutions. How easy to make Ben the villain.

She frowns uncomfortably. She's concerned.

"One needn't always be straightforward!" I hiss advisedly. Then racing, I lock myself in the bedroom as she opens the front door wide.

Rennie Williams arrives, stamping his feet, tramping off snow, which dissolves, patting his dog who shakes roughly and sniffs my cat, lolling out a pink tongue. The cat hides under a chair. His friend, a stubby dark-haired man with a white smile, takes off his leather jacket and muffler and both he and Rennie begin beaming, looking around, fingering my paintings, patting the furniture, squatting at the book-shelves and rocking on their heels to see my taste.

I watch from a crack in the door, behind a drape. Rennie is astonished to find me not home. I'd told him I was sick. "And the thing is, I couldn't find her phone listed anywhere in the phone book. I had no choice. I hope she's not mad that I came, but I brought this."

"Why should she be mad?" Anna takes their coats, then unsure where to hang them, standing with her spine straight, she gives them back, not wanting to be accused of stealing, or to get bogged down.

Rennie opens the shopping bags and takes out food, lots of food, wrapped in newspaper over tinfoil, hunks of beef and steaming brown rice with gravy, mashed potatoes and cranberries, savory pork stew, thick and rich. He shrugs. His shoulders are thick and wide. "I guess I'll leave this then, you don't think she'll mind if I leave some food. Shall I leave the plates too?" He taps a finger to his tooth, uncertainly.

"If you want to," Anna says stolidly, unsure herself. She glances hesitantly at the bedroom door. "There must be more aluminum foil here someplace. She has plates, I know. We'll look for them."

They all disappear into the kitchen through the archway, the dog too, wagging his silky tail. Finally my little cat, too curious, unable to resist following, slinks along behind them. I hear doors opening, slamming, cabinets, the metal ones beneath the sink.

"It doesn't make any difference," Rennie's voice is saying. The refrigerator sighs, then heaves, then hums. They talk more softly. I can't make them out. Then, clearly: "I'll leave the dishes. She can return them later."

For one moment I'm afraid Anna will ask them to stay, invite them to dine with her out of obligation. But she's too polite for that, she owes her foremost debt to me. And I, despite my interest, because of it—who knows?—worry suddenly that Rennie seems too good-natured, maybe he's ignorant on purpose, deliberately taking his time, and what would I say if he discovers me now. He has a dog. He could smell me out. But I can make up a good excuse, be plausible, if necessary. Too bad I've got to wish him away.

His flushed face comes back in view.

Anna invites them to sit and wait. But Rennie refuses, turning ruddy palms up, saying there's no point. Only his dog sits. It sprawls and whines. Rennie snaps his fingers. The dog gets up. After a short while amidst merry goodbyes and Happy New Years' and regrets, Rennie turns in a tight circle at the door, awkward at admitting failure again, reluctant, but then adamantly grabs the knob. The dog barks.

Inside the bedroom, I'm relieved. But all at once, even though I know Rennie's gone, a hand larger than life, a wrist with a leather wristband, thrusts in at me through the crack. The bedroom door bursts open. Rennie's friend, a handsome Chicano I see up close, comes after me and yells, "Got you! I've got you now!" He won't let me go. "Man, I knew it, I knew it! I knew there was something fishy. Rennie!" He grips me, elated. He's been sliding forward against the wall, out of my line of vision, waiting for me. He runs to the window and flings it open, levering the sash high with his shoulder, holding on to me. He lets in freezing air. "I had a hunch. Rennie! Rennie!" He's laughing hard.

But Rennie is gone already. His big footprints are indistinguishable in the snow from the rest. So are the dog's pads. The streets are being shoveled, we hear the scraping. It's growing late. Cars, muffled, drive curiously slow. A brown haze descends over the pink lamplight. Rennie is gone. Irretrievable.

"Did you see all the food they brought us?" Anna says. The food smells delicious, oniony, heavy, hearty—not Balducci's or Dean and De Luca's gourmet fare, but down-homecooking, from Midwest farms. Did Rennie cook it himself? "Of course with your flu you probably can't eat it. It would lay in your stomach like a lead weight."

Strangely, for the first time in weeks, I'm starving though.

"He's an awfully nice boy, that Rennie."

"Couldn't be bigger or better." The Chicano friend claps his hands.

But instead of going into the dining room and setting out the food, we eat it off the silver-trimmed platters Rennie brought, right at the kitchen counter with big soup spoons, then finally dipping in with our hands. I try to speak more formally to compensate for this. "Rennie'*sh* generoshity overwhelm*sh* me," I slush. "Really, I hardly knew him, he wa*sh* my friend'*sh* friend." I strive now for crispness. "Have you known him long?"

But I turn away from his answer. What if I imagine Ben coming home from work right now? Even though this is my sleepless dream in which Anna as I imagine her is the reality—my opposite, my mirror self—I worry about interruptions. It's time. I eat faster and faster. Everyone is eating too fast, we're stuffing up. But what's this? In the bottom of a dish, soggy, covered up by rice, is a long envelope, a buckled surprise: two $25 gift certificates from D'Agostino's Grocery Store too. One for me; one for Anna.

Wait! I'm indignant. The gifts frighten me. *Who's who?* I'm not needy! I'm in control.

"Listen," I say between bites, unable to stop gorging. "We have to return these gift certificates right away."

"Why?" Anna demands petulantly. "Why do we? It's not fair. Why? Why?"

"Because we're not entitled to them, of course," I say, swallowing.

And because I'm the one with a home and she isn't—*how
should I know the answers? whose fault is it, not mine!*—I
banish her downstairs again with a hot thermos. I lock the
door. I'm still sick, so I belch.

For the moment, I feel lonely, abandoned almost, but
I'm safer.

DAYS OF THE DEAD

Through the tinted window, the Mexican hillsides were green. The rainy season had just ended. Cactuses were in bloom, all kinds, long cactuses and squat ones, and rangy cactuses with cottony limbs. Goats and donkeys munched grass by the road. In the front of the bus, a pretty long-haired bus attendant in a tight red miniskirt and jacket passed out soft drinks and sandwiches. Charlotte knew that if her father were alive at this moment he'd be flirting with that bus attendant. But her father had died three years ago of a heart attack on a bus out of Mexico City on his way to San Miguel. And now Charlotte was riding one of those same roomy, luxury buses, with miniature TV sets playing movies overhead, mimicking an airline. Charlotte was traveling to San Miguel to celebrate the Days of the Dead. Inside her purse, she carried a handful of ashes—her father's ashes. She was tracking her father's path, three years too late.

Jordan, her husband, slouched in the seat next to Charlotte, didn't seem to notice the sexy young bus attendant at all. His honorable blue-eyed gaze was fixed on Charlotte—as it should be, but often wasn't after eleven years.

"How're you doing?" Jordan looped a thick arm around
Charlotte's neck, and with his other hand, accepted a sandwich from the bus attendant. He peeled the top slice of
bread back to sniff.

"I'm fine." Charlotte stared out the window.

At some point in his journey—was it here?—Charlotte's
mother said that her father had gasped, dropped the book
he was reading, and toppled out of his seat.

Charlotte's father had always joked about death. "Throw
my body in the garbage when I die." He was proud of shun-
ning "the hollow religious rituals," if not the culture, of his
forebears. A phony bravado, Charlotte thought. Like most
people, could he imagine dying? And when he had died in
Mexico, unexpectedly, could even he have imagined the
international complications, the problem of shipping his
body back? No hometown rabbi would preside over serv-
ices for her father when her mother returned with the ashes.
Cremation was against Jewish tradition.

The bus stopped to re-fuel. Charlotte raked short curls
out of her eyes. A street peddler draped in Day of the Dead
baubles ran alongside, the driver handed out money, then
hooked a dangling skeleton next to a Virgin of Guadelupe
on a large rear-view mirror that proclaimed *¡Hola!*

Tomorrow, on the Day of the Dead, Charlotte would
bury her father's ashes in San Miguel, the town that he
loved. If indeed these were his ashes. She'd heard stories
about these cremations, how the bones of all different people get mixed up and the ashes you end up with could be
anyone's—not necessarily her father's. Though in that case
maybe a mix-up would appeal to him, his sense of irony,
fervent internationalist that he was, believer in mixing up
boundaries. Death was the most clearly defined boundary
she knew. Charlotte would love to mix Death up.

But she wasn't going to mention the ashes to Jordan again. She and Jordan had argued about the ashes last night. Jordan was sympathetic to Charlotte's intentions, he'd said, but not to her deed. Charlotte had lifted the ashes from her mother's house. Only a handful. They wouldn't be missed. Her mother kept the ashes in an urn shaped like a loving cup on a closet shelf, shoved behind shoeboxes filled with important papers. The urn was plastic, gold and gray, really tacky. Even in dealing with death, her mother was cheap. Charlotte's father had been the opposite, naturally expansive. So was Jordan, Charlotte thought—when he didn't stop and think.

Maybe Jordan was right, not about her theft but his crack that it was fitting for her father to be encased in plastics. Her father was stuck in plastics for most of his life. After inventing a fume-free styrofoam molding and cutting machine, he had landed a job in North Carolina at a Christmas novelties plant owned by another New York Jew who read about his invention in an industrial magazine. Carl Marks was the name of his employer—a name that made Charlotte's family smile because her father occasionally professed Communist sympathies. Charlotte remembered watching him scratch his prickly moustache. "How did it happen? I work for *Das Kapital*-ist now."

Jordan nudged Charlotte to pay attention to him.

"'On the Day of the Dead, the departed can return,'" Jordan read to Charlotte from his underlined tourist guide. Jordan was treating this whole trip as a tourist excursion.

"Good." Charlotte cut him off because today she wasn't in the mood for a reasonable discussion.

Today, her whole relationship with Jordan seemed too reasonable.

I want my father back.

Charlotte still recalled her disbelief when her mother had phoned, speaking in a high, breathy voice from the American Embassy, telling Charlotte that Mexican officials needed to be bribed to release the body. "Charlotte, our Daddy is dead. Our Daddy is gone—" As if he were her father too.

"Face it," Charlotte told Jordan outright last night in a moment of wry confession about her topsy-turvy little girl's passion. "You're no substitute for my father."

"Face it." Jordan was equally wry, with a rare trace of bitterness. "Even your real father is no substitute for your *father.*"

"You're the one who understands me better than anyone else, better than your mother," her father used to tell her during their late-night conversations in the kitchen after everyone else was asleep, conversations that always started out about Charlotte's ideas, Charlotte's problems, Charlotte's needs, and ended up about him—conversations, Jordan joked, that had softened Charlotte up for all the married men she later met before Jordan who never had wives who understood them either.

"You know why I think you're so beautiful," her father used to croon, stroking her chin before he left her to sleep with his wife. "I think you're beautiful because you're mine . . . ."

And remembering, Charlotte felt sad and angry. She wondered, glaring out at the desert mountains they were passing, if she should consider throwing his ashes out the window instead.

Yet unburied, her father still had a hold on her life, like one of his pouncing tricks, where he'd grip her at a pres-

sure point on her wrist, and paralyze her, and tickle her
side until she gave up.

"Mom!" she'd yell.

"Murray, let her go! What are you trying to prove, that
you're stronger than a ten-year old girl? Don't tease."

He was a dark, wiry, playful man, completely different as
a good-looking type from Jordan, who was broad and light.

The bus arrived in San Miguel. Charlotte and Jordan
took a cab to a hotel that was pink and fancy.

They unpacked and made love, an ordinary couple on
vacation. Then Jordan fell asleep. He snored, oblivious to
Charlotte's wakefulness, his large body sprawled over the
bed. He was exhausted from the bus trip, and the long day.
Charlotte looked down at her husband, thought about his
reasonableness, and brushed a flap of hair from over his
eye. He had beautiful eyes. He had beautiful cheekbones.
Jordan might not be surprised to hear that he was still her
father's rival. But Jordan had been surprised—and more
than a little pleased, she guessed—by the primal way she'd
nipped at his flesh earlier in this bed, displaying her teeth.

She had been visualizing skull teeth in skull racks in the
Mexico City Anthropology Museum while their limbs were
entwining. She and Jordan had visited that museum at the
start of their trip. Next to the skull racks had stood a
receptacle for hearts ripped from sacrificial victims.

Hadn't her father acted like she was ripping his heart out
years ago when she married Jordan? "I'm happy because
you're happy," he'd sing-songed grimly, pinching her cheek
too hard.

Jordan sometimes threw that memory into her face.
Jordan claimed that Charlotte had only hooked up with
him after a disastrous marriage to a terrible architect, a
man Charlotte had picked up at twenty-one because she

knew she'd better marry someone soon to make a break with her father—and when that first husband became a Jew for Jesus, he reminded her how her father had criticized her for a ridiculous choice.

"I thought you were supposed to be so smart!" her father had said. "How could you leave me for a creep like that?"

But that's the point! she'd wanted to shout at him. Back then Charlotte was going not just for second-best, but for fortieth or fiftieth-best. *It was a way of fooling myself, Daddy. Not really breaking with you at all.*

In the morning they hired a taxi and visited the town next to San Miguel and the Museum of the Mummies that Jordan read about, which turned out not to feature real mummies at all but poor Indians buried in the municipal cemetery whose families could no longer afford to pay the small land fee each year to rent their graves. They'd been dug up, evicted, and—preserved by chemicals in the soil— displayed in glass cases with tiny satin pillows under their heads. The child-mummies wore crowns and tattered cloaks like saints, the men's penis sacks flopped off to one side, and the women's breasts were leathery folds. The mummies grinned like a cheap Hollywood horror movie, mouths agape, as if in screams.

Charlotte turned to Jordan. He, however, was turning pale. Oh, my God. Would he faint? If *she* fainted Jordan would throw her over his shoulder like a sack of grain and carry her to safety. It had happened once at a party. But if *Jordan* fainted, what would *she* do?

"The mummies' expressions are from tendon shrinkage, Jordan." Charlotte steadied her voice. It came out sounding sarcastic. "It's not a comment on death. It's not from pain."

Then she steadied Jordan too, and led him down the Museum hallways where male and female skeletons frolicked in comic Day of the Dead engravings lining the wall.

"How do you know?" Jordan's voice was wary.

"Science. College biology class." Charlotte jabbed him lightly in the ribs. "What is this, some kind of turnaround? Suddenly I'm the reasonable one?"

Outside, Jordan straightened his meaty shoulders. He was embarrassed about his queasiness, but Charlotte realized that she didn't mind a brief glimpse of his weakness at all. Usually he was unflappable, and she, the intense, unpredictable spouse. Later, they window-shopped, looked at the Mexican Bridge of Sighs, and ate *moles* for lunch. Then they taxied back to San Miguel.

There, in the city Charlotte's father so loved, the *Todos Santos* activities were in full swing. The whole town was decorated in Day of the Dead cutouts. Yet a woman in a business suit at the Tourist Office, who looked as though she'd stepped out of the pages of Mexican Vogue, was evasive about the location of the Indian vigils. Only superstitious Indians celebrated the occasion, she said. On the street, children swung hollowed-out jack o'lanterns at them, begging for coins.

"Do you think she was trying to stop us?"

"If it was a warning, it was wasted on me." Jordan tapped his tourist book.

"What does that mean?"

It meant he had a good sense of direction. He would put it to use.

The sun was sliding in and out behind clouds when they joined a long line of families snaking their way to the muncipal cemetery, which was called the Pantheon, at the edge of town. Jordan strapped a little plastic canteen of purified water to his belt. It was a hot dusty day, and celebrants carried marigolds, magenta coxcombs, palm leaves, bougainvilleas, or wreathes of moss. Charlotte bought a bouquet of marigolds.

Jordan looked pleased with himself. "We must be getting close."

Jordan consulted the book and they squeezed into an alley stuffed with food stands and exuberant balloons. Indian women hawked *pan de muerte* and sugar skulls bearing individuals' names.

"*Dos cinquentos, dos cinquentos!*" Flower sellers shouted.

"Festive mourners," Jordan grinned with sweaty tourist brightness.

The crowd pushed. They surged forward.

"Watch out!"

The crowd pressed Charlotte and Jordan together, and against a wire-mesh fence. Charlotte clutched her purse. Any snatcher would be disappointed because everything was in her moneybelt except for a comb, lipstick, and a baggie of the ashes. "Do you think we should go in now or wait until the mob thins?"

"Too late to turn back."

"You're right. More people trying to get in than trying to leave."

"Isn't it always that way with graveyards?" Jordan teased.

They passed through a turnstile. Between lavish botanical displays and simple wooden crosses on gravesites so close you had to tread on them to move at all, descendants of the dead milled and knotted in a brilliant delirium. Children wormed around Charlotte and Jordan hauling tin soup cans filled with water from a public faucet. Skinny grandmothers tilted sideways with the weight of their heavy pails.

"Look, they're planting flowers." Jordan pointed at families pick-axing their plots. Some families exhibited photos of the departed. Others decorated their plots like little shrines.

Charlotte said, "And they're scattering flowers."

She and Jordan tried threading their way out of the crowd to a main path hedged with trash-cans. The trash-cans were overflowing with piles of yesterday's blooms.

An old Indian man wove past them. He plunged his arms into one of the trash-cans and sorted through throwaways. Many discarded flowers were still vivid. The old man flung loose a bough of bougainvilleas and smoothed out bedraggled gladiolus trumpeting life. They watched him head purposefully across the cemetery, wearing an expression of triumph.

Jordan rubbed his brow. "Too poor to buy flowers. Not too poor to make a graveside offering at some family site of his own."

"The people can be poor in material goods but rich in spirit." Old familiar words popped out of Charlotte. One of her father's clichés. She felt her cheeks grow pink.

"Big hands, big feet! I want you girls to notice the way Mexican artists show you the dignity of the people," her father used to exhort. She had grown up with prints of Diego Rivera's peasants and Orozco's *campesinos* toiling in the living-room. "Charlotte, I want you and your sister to learn moral priorities. Forget about race, forget about class, forget nationalities. Everybody is one in the eyes of Time."

Her father always said Time where others said God. Before her father had taken that job at the Christmas novelties company, he had been a political activist, what he liked to call "a free spirit," and free-lance inventor, stinking up the kitchen with his experiments on the stove. "Patent pending!" he shouted when her mother squawked. Now her mother lived on the income from his stinking experiments.

But the patent for his biggest moneymaker—the fume-free styrofoam molder—was owned by the novelties company in the South. Her father had traded it for a regular paycheck. "A man's got to grow up, he's got to put food on his family's table."

It all sounded so corny now. Maybe Charlotte had replayed the words too often.

Her father had said, "I won't be a wage slave forever. Your old man will surprise you—and I'll surprise myself too, one day."

So Charlotte had waited to be surprised. Jordan said she was kidding herself. Patient Griselda, he called her. Jordan liked her father but the time her father tried the paralyzing pouncing trick on Jordan's wrist, Jordan hadn't been paralyzed. The trick didn't work. Charlotte's father looked confused. He was a man accustomed to displaying powers around his family, but around Jordan, he seemed jittery. "He's a nice man, gentle," her father had whispered a month before she got married. "He might be too gentle for you."

She and Jordan had just celebrated their seventh anniversary when a large Taiwanese conglomerate bought out the Christmas novelties company. Her father was fired with a small sum of severance. "Not exactly a golden handshake, or even a silver one, but maybe a tin one," he'd cracked, staving off his daughter's concern—"something more akin to the materials of the poor Mexican artisan's spirit." He was fifty-nine years old. He didn't want sympathy. Within a month he'd moved to San Miguel, enrolled in the *Instituto de Arte*, and taught himself to sculpt with clay. The heft of clays rejuvenated him, although he had already developed arthritis, lost flexibility in his hands.

"Do you know what I dreamed last night?" he said over a fading phone line from Mexico City the last time they talked. "I was living in an beautiful underground city, all clay. I had molded all the houses and buildings myself. It was a special kind of clay. It cured arthritis. I was strong as a horse in that dream, completely flexible, spinning like a dancer. When I woke up, I realized there must be a way to infuse ordinary clay with heat to treat people with the same problem as mine. A formula. Something in capsules that bursts with heat when you knead it. I worked out the ingredients. I came up with it too. You see, my formula could be a breakthrough."

"Patent pending," Charlotte murmured in the graveyard. Jordan tilted his head at her, quizzically.

"What's this business with tearing up different-colored flower petals?" Jordan peered at mourners bending to sprinkle *campasuchil*, fragrant trails, around the graves. "I thought people were just supposed to create flower paths in their homes around their altars."

"The paths are markers. If the dead get confused and can't find their way back to their graves they might cause trouble for the living."

"Ghosts?"

"Something like that." No grave, no flowers. No wonder her father lost his way back to her.

"Jordan, do you think it's okay we're here? Maybe we're intruding." Charlotte remembered the chic woman in the Tourist Office. "We're the only gringos in sight."

"It's fine."

"Then I want to bury my father's ashes here now."

"Here now?" Jordan stopped, exasperated. Two small girls in party dresses and ribbons walking behind them bumped into Jordan and ran away. Charlotte waited for Jordan to go pale as he had that morning. Instead, Jordan alarmed her by turning red. "You need a permit to bury him in this graveyard. This is the municipal cemetery. There's not enough space, just look around. I thought you were going to scatter him in the central plaza, in the *Jardin*—"

"Too touristy," Charlotte shrugged. That had been the plan she'd thrown at Jordan after his queasiness at the Museum of the Mummies, when the timing had been right for enlisting his support. When the music was playing, she'd said, they'd scatter the ashes by the bandstand. Her father would get a real send-off. But now Charlotte was stirred by the pageantry of all these grieving mourners. She was grieving too. Her father ought to end up in a dignified place. She pictured the *Jardin* with its dense plane trees, dispirited mariachi players and car traffic circling, on one side armed police with bandoliers and ragged Indian-rights protesters on the other. "It's too polluted there, too busy. He'll be kicked under taxis and out into the street."

"But it's more crowded here. Here, today, everybody will be walking on him."

"I don't think he'd mind. He always identified with the downtrodden."

She waited for Jordan to smile. Jordan didn't.

Charlotte's father would have loved it, though. Around the house, he always teased and bragged and strutted. In the heat of summer he stripped down to his jockey shorts, even answering the door that way, occasionally forgetting and snapping the waistband while he talked.

"Murray, get out of the doorway! People are looking at you."

"Let them look. What do I care?" he'd say, while Charlotte and her sister huddled, giggling. They were thrilled by his audacity. Maybe that's why men had families. Captive audiences.

"Then just get it over with," Jordan said. "Dump the damned ashes."

Charlotte winced. "Maybe I ought to dump you."

"You know, you really are a genius at picking a place to fight. We travel all the way here and I do everything you want because I know this is some kind of big psychological deal for you, but the first time I don't want to go along with your crazy scheme you threaten to leave. Well, what if I left? You and your father. You don't need me."

"Hey," Charlotte said. She was hurt. "I didn't know you thought my plans to bury my father were a scheme."

Jordan snorted. That made her mad.

She said, "You missed the point."

"What point?"

"I have to do this right."

"There is no right way to bury somebody. He's dead. You loved him. He was your father. That's always going to feel wrong."

She stalked away from Jordan fast, crisscrossing gravesites.

He followed. He grabbed for her.

She ducked. "Besides, you owe me an apology. I see a perfectly good space for burying him."

She stabbed her thumb at a corner far off the main path, a plot of dry earth where no one was standing.

"No, you can't bury him there." Jordan zigzagged. He eyed the site. "It's already a grave."

She shot him a wary look. She sidled towards the plot herself and squinted at a granite marker. Spidery words in English were chipped into stone: *Sadye Levy, 1919-1979. She loved all and was loved by all.* Next to the name was a small Star of David.

"Oh, Jordan! What am I going to do?" Frustration welled up and made Charlotte weepy. "I'll never find a place for him, will I? And wouldn't you know it? The woman who is buried here was Jewish, the same as he was."

Jordan nodded, noncommittal. That was just like him, he was still reaching for her hand. "Check out that fancy spelling of Sadie."

"It's an old-fashioned name, a leftover from an earlier generation—" She yanked it away.

"Leftover Sadye," he said, without skipping a beat. He stared at the plot. "Probably an American who died here with no family to take care of her grave."

Charlotte looked down too. She spotted the bones scattered on the top of the grave a second after he did. Human bones stained almost the same color as the earth, large fragments except for two long thick bones with bifurcated knobs on top like anatomy class photos of thighbones, one snapped in half and jagged, the other strewn but intact.

"Are they . . . do you think . . . they're Sadye's bones?" Her heart dove, as if pounced upon, in her chest.

"Probably," Jordan nodded.

At an adjoining site, a teenaged boy in a white dress shirt pulled away from his family and dropped onto all fours. He kicked and scraped the dirt from a slab with such violent speed that Charlotte thought he must be throwing a temper tantrum.

She felt dizzy, weak, another pounce in her chest. A life was a small thing. These bones once inhabited it.

"Let's cover her up. It's not right for her bones to be lying out here, naked and broken. Let's cover her with more flowers from the trashcan." She flung down her marigolds. They barely hid one of the shattered fragments. Maybe something about this was a message from her father. Crazy idea! Her father would have pooh- poohed it. Listlessly, Charlotte shoved dirt with her foot.

"How about if we leave the cemetery and buy more flowers—"

"No, that will take too long. The trashcan." She raised her voice.

Jordan frowned but didn't budge.

Locals who had politely averted their eyes turned from nearby gravesites and stared.

"Then I'll do it, Jordan. You stay here and guard the grave."

"Guard the grave?"

She straightened slowly, wondering why Jordan looked surprised and not disturbed by the bones the way he had been by the naked mummies this morning, and then realized that she'd just used a childish expression ("Guard the fort! Guard the wagons! Guard the dolls!"), a throwback to games with her family. She lurched forward, began striding—what Jordan dubbed her "window-shaking stride"—thumping the earth so hard and moving so fast that she had to switch back and forth and step around. So many mourners everywhere! They seemed to be swirling, faces popping out at her as she tried to squeeze past. Heat and dust pressed on her. She was dazed, dazzled, enclosed in a kaleidoscope of colors. It seemed like blind luck when she finally found the path with its trashcans overflowing with flowers.

Since she'd passed the trashcans earlier, mourners had thrown their old food on top of the garbage heap, and she swept the top layer right off with the flowers. She didn't know why she felt this need to keep a stranger's bones from abandonment. But it didn't matter where the flowers came from. *Throw my body in the garbage when I'm done,* her father had told her. Then her world tipped over, one glorious globe-sized dump.

Charlotte? her father's voice whispered.

She swiveled around, looking for him. She could picture him perfectly—hear his sarcastic asides, his dry cough, see his eyebrows arching when he went to make change for a twenty at the gas station and, unable to grasp it, watched the wind blow the money from his arthritic hand.

Of course, he wasn't there.

And she'd lost sight of Jordan too. She clutched old dying flowers, a giant heap, precariously in her arms. She peered around them. It wasn't the first time she'd gotten lost, confused about which way to go. Jordan sometimes made fun of her for this.

But it wasn't Jordan's fault she'd gotten lost. It was her own—or maybe her father's. He used to like to steer her forward, or sideways, or backwards. When she was little she loved when he walked behind her, with his big hands around her waist.

Charlotte stood on tiptoes, panicking a little, scanning for Jordan. What if he'd fainted? Then she thought of how red he had turned. Oh, shit! That had been stupid of her to pick a fight. What if he had a heart attack, like her father? Jordan was such a big man—tall, not too muscular, not too stout—and Charlotte felt certain that she ought to be able to spot the gold gleam of his hair. He ought to be the highest human point in the cemetery. But looking around, she saw that many Mexican men in the Pantheon wore straw hats that made them tall.

"Charlotte!"

Her eye was caught by something, something above, whipping the dust, splitting the air, gripping her fingers. She couldn't move. She was paralyzed even as she noticed Jordan twenty feet away, loping towards her, grumpily, from the opposite direction.

Jordan called, "Where the hell have you been?"

"Duck!" She heard a buzzing rasp. Something was out of control. "It's my father, Jordan!"

Jordan flung his arm up as if protecting himself.

Bue he was only waving, reaching for her, then pulling up alongside, hugging her tight. "What's going on? Why are you acting crazy? I think you're having a panic reaction. Sweetie, if this is just a one-time event, I'll get you more flowers from the garbage can."

He was bargaining with her. He held onto her all the way back to the trashcan where he scooped flowers, and all the way back to Sadye Levy's gravesite.

Jordan hurled his flowers over the bones. He pitched them with a wild energy that took Charlotte by surprise. Red dust smudged his face. They crouched, not exactly praying, and not exactly meditating, although Charlotte whispered a few words of Kaddish. She unzipped her purse. The ashes were twisted in a plastic baggie. She untied the baggie. She dipped her hand into it and held the ashes for a long time, grinding them into her palm. The ashes were gritty. Jordan shook her shoulder. He wanted her to let go.

Charlotte turned the baggie upside-down and the ashes fell loose. A breeze suspended them for a moment, swept particles of her father against her, and then the ashes dropped and spread onto the loose earth. Charlotte bent and mixed her hands in ashes and soil, and then mixed the ashes and soil together with Sadye Levy's bones. She picked up a bone. The bones felt light. Charlotte felt light, as if the ashes had been weighing her down.

She and Jordan buried the ashes alongside the bones.

Jordan sighed. "This gravesite will certainly get dug up again."

Charlotte guessed that he was probably right.

She looked around. At the cemetery's perimeter boys were whitewashing crypts, inscribing names on freshly-laid plaster with broken twigs. In New York City, her home, these boys would be inscribing graffiti in hallways. For a moment, for a few moments, she had brushed up against another world. When Charlotte focused on Jordan again, she could tell from his expression that he was contemplating his strangeness here the same way she was, the fact that they were strangers, strangers to each other, and tourists in the land of the living, scuttling through sights.

Jordan wiped his hands on his pants. They left the gravesite.

"Most markers," Jordan was explaining, cleaning dirt and ashes from under his fingernails as they passed fresh crowds pushing in for Day of the Dead, "have the word *refrescado* and a date painted on the back. Not hers. Our gal Sadye didn't pay the rent."

They stopped before they left the cemetery at the public faucet near the turnstile to wash their hands. Jordan unsnapped the plastic water canteen from his belt.

He hoisted the canteen at Charlotte. "To your father," he toasted. He passed her the purified water. "You did right by him, Charlotte, even if we argued about it. You made his trip."

"Yeah, but the handful of ashes I brought with me are only a small part of his remains."

Jordan smacked his hand humorously against his forehead. "At this rate you can go on burying him for the rest of your life."

"It might take that long." Charlotte sipped from the canteen.

Some children pushed by and splashed into the faucet. The sun coasted free of a cloud and little prisms of light danced on water droplets. Charlotte recognized that feeling again, like a phantom heartbeat. Something was loosening its hold.